Acclaim for
Come Tomorrow You'll Regret Today:
Collected Stories

"In concise, unadorned prose, Patrick Trotti considers the pain and crisis of our American moment. Trotti's taut collection is a tender meditation on the quiet uncertainties of life. While those uncertainties have the power to overwhelm, for Trotti, they also have the potential to inspire, bewilder and delight. There are no answers here, only shattering and glorious questions. Trotti's stories are a triumph of restraint and invention."

- Amber Dermont, New York Times *bestselling author of* The Starboard Sea

"In sentences of perfect economy, Trotti has unveiled something truly frightening. I was sometimes left so sad reading these stories, I found myself repeating my favorite phrases, consoling myself by letting it happen again. I wanted more and more."

- Richard Chiem, author of You Private Person

"Patrick Trotti's collection, *Come Tomorrow You'll Regret Today,* is a quite wonderful cross-section of stories wrought from the imagination of a writer in full command of his craft. Trotti takes the reader from the lofty heights of superhero worship to the depths of painful loss, never skipping a beat, never faltering in his trajectory. Trotti writes modern day parables of longing, loss, and desire, all-the-while infusing these stories with a wit and wisdom not often seen in much of today's fiction."

- *James Claffey, author of* Blood A Cold Blue

COME TOMORROW YOU'LL REGRET TODAY

collected stories

PATRICK TROTTI

TAILWINDS PRESS

Tailwinds Press
P.O. Box 2283, Radio City Station
New York, NY 10101-2283
www.tailwindspress.com

Published in the United States of America
ISBN: 978-0-9904546-2-5
1st ed. June 2015

Contents

COME
TOMORROW
YOU'LL REGRET
TODAY

PART ONE

ZIPPY LINCOLN

For one day in fourth grade I had a black beard and a top hat. Neither were mine but that didn't matter.

It was the first school-related competition that I'd won. I didn't get a ribbon or medal like the spelling bee winners or those laminated proclamations for the kid who has perfect attendance. I got a black top hat, a fake black beard from my teacher, and a black suit and shoes that my mom went to Sears to get.

The only reason I entered the contest was because we shared the same birthday. I looked it up in the library one day when the weather was so bad that we weren't even allowed outside for lunch. It was Lincoln, Charles Darwin, and Arsenio Hall. I hated science and I wasn't black, or funny, so all I had was Abe.

In the next town over they had a memorial for Lincoln. Apparently he had come through this area and made a speech. There was a statue on the side of the road. I only saw it as we zoomed by in the car. It was at the top of the hill that entered the town where all the violence happened and the drug dealers were. That's what I heard my mom say over the phone one day.

It came down to this girl and me. I wasn't expecting to win, but once I found out that I was down to the final two, I wanted to win. I thought it would be funny, and a bit weird, if the girl had to wear a beard and act like an old man. The year before we did something similar for Susan B. Anthony and we all made fun of this boy just because he finished second. If he'd won and worn a wig and a dress, we would've ragged on him for the rest of the year.

I thought I was in trouble when my teacher called me out into the hallway. I swallowed my gum. She was a real nasty lady. I'd gotten detention for chewing gum in class. When I got outside, she closed the door. A girl in my grade was already out there, leaning up against the wall. She was a real dork. I'd never even talked to her before so I knew that I wasn't in trouble.

"Congratulations to both of you. You two are the finalists for our Lincoln recital."

The teacher bent down to eye level with us. She had a huge smile on her face. She looked like one of those old people in the movies who gave out treats to her grandkids because she didn't know what else to do. I thought she was going to rub my hair or pinch my cheek.

"Next week I'm going to have both of you perform in front of the class. They'll get a say in who wins, but it'll be up to me in the end."

"Good luck."

The girl was turned towards me with her hand out. It was the first time I'd heard her speak outside of class. We shook hands and went back into class.

When I told my friends about it at lunch, I was ready for them to start making fun of me. They did for a bit, but then they told me that I had to win. That I was representing all the boys in our class, and that if I lost out on playing a man to a girl, I should be ashamed of myself. They said that it would've been worse than if our buddy had won last year and played the woman.

"We never win anything. Think about it, the only time we get mentioned at school is when we get in trouble. This would be the first good thing for you, for all of us, at school. We could actually say that we won something. And it's not like you have to take some difficult test or anything. Just memorize a speech. It's easy dude."

They were all looking at me. I'd only seen that look on their faces, in their eyes, when we were on the basketball court or baseball diamond. It took a lot for them to get excited, especially if it had to do with school.

"Alright, alright, I'll win, don't worry. Just lay off it already. We're starting to sound like the nerd table. Let's just talk about something else."

They did, for a while. They'd bring it up here and there. They even called me Abe for the next few days until the finals.

My mom was just as excited. She called in and asked for the day off from work. Although I told her I hadn't won yet, she said that didn't matter, that it was just a formality. I didn't share her optimism, but for once she wasn't mad at me when talking about school, so I stayed quiet.

Each night before bed I recited the speech into the mirror. I kept my door closed. The second night my mom opened the door in the middle of the speech. She sat down on my bed and watched. I continued with the speech. Every few sentences I would look over to find her nodding along, that same smile that the teacher had plastered on her face. I could see my dirty magazines poking out from under my mattress as she fidgeted about on my bed.

We had to perform on a Friday. It was mid-January.

"Okay class, settle down. Today we're going to have our two finalists for the Lincoln recital perform their speeches for you. At the end, everyone will vote for who they think should win. Now pay attention and keep quiet. These two have worked very hard at this."

A collective giggle went through the class.

I went first. When the teacher introduced me, all of my friends stood up and started to cheer loudly like when we went to the Garden that year to watch Jordan play the Knicks. They were all seated in the back two rows of the class. The teacher had to yell at them to get them to stop.

I was almost perfect. I took my time and only had to look down at the speech once. I was loud enough that people passing by in the hall could hear me.

My friends jumped up at the end, this time even louder with their applause. Our teacher looked at them and then at me and just shook her head. She waited for them to stop cheering and yelling, which didn't happen until I reached my seat.

She introduced the girl and the girls in the class started to cheer. It wasn't nearly as loud. But it wasn't as obnoxious as the boys; it was more refined. She rushed through her speech, looking down at the paper every few sentences. She even stumbled pronouncing a few words. She spoke barely above a whisper. If I hadn't just finished reciting the same speech, I wouldn't have been able to follow her. She took about half as long as me and didn't wait for any applause. She put her head down and rushed back to her seat. Some of the girls clapped but all of the boys remained silent. I knew I had won. The voting was just to confirm what we all knew already.

The only downside to winning was that I had to perform on my birthday. That should've been obvious but it was the last thing that came to mind. Instead of enjoying my birthday by just zoning out at school, I had to get up on a wooden box and recite the Gettysburg Address in front of our entire elementary school. Some parents also showed up, as well as people from the town. I just remember a lot of old people who got dropped off by a different type of bus than the one we rode in to and from school.

It was cold and windy. One hand was on my top hat and the other was scratching my beard. It felt like Velcro around my mouth. I kept on getting the ends of the hair on my tongue. I was so cold and distracted that I didn't have the time to become nervous. I had the entire speech memorized anyway. It was one of the last times that I really gave my best effort at something school-related.

My class was standing in the front row with my teacher. A guy from the local newspaper was there with a camera and notepad. He took a bunch of photos. I could hear some of my friends laughing every few words. I tried to take my time but I rushed through it because I wanted to get the suit jacket off and put on my winter jacket.

I finished and got a good ovation. My teacher looked proud, and so did my mom. I stepped off of the box and brushed by the Principal. I rushed over to my friends; my hat was already in my hands with the beard in it. After the Principal talked, the Mayor took the microphone and went on about the proud history of the area and the future being our kids. It sounded like something someone his age would say.

I asked my best friend how I did and he couldn't stop laughing. The teacher even gave us a look, that type where they're almost looking through you. He stopped, but I waited for his answer.

"Look down."

"What?"

"Your pants, look," he said.

My fly was down. It'd been unzipped the whole time.

They were already coming up with nicknames. Zippy Lincoln was the one they deemed the best.

I never left my house in the morning without double-checking my fly after that.

WAL-MART COLLEGE

They gave me a choice. At least according to them. Some choice, work or school. More specifically: get a job, save up some money, and move out on my own, or enroll in college and continue living at home rent-free.

Laziness governed my choice. Just thinking about packing up my stuff and moving and trying to fill up an entire apartment with things made me tired. I wanted a nap, and not a quick power nap but one of those great long slumbering, dead to the world, four-hour-long naps.

Choosing college made my mom happy. A lifetime of academia had softened her, making her a *de facto* champion of the benefits of higher education. My dad, on the other hand, suspected I was up to something. Projecting his college experience onto me, he silently brooded over my decision, imagining endless frat parties, keg stands, and a minimal course load.

That weekend my mom went to Barnes & Noble and brought home a stack of materials concerning college. She quietly laid them on the top step leading up to my room, her way of signaling its importance. The enormity of the data was too much to process. Endless rankings, lists of requirements, majors offered, and financial aid packages overwhelmed me. I put the magazines away, locked my door, and played Xbox—making sure to keep the volume turned down.

The deadline imposed by my father for coming up with a final list of schools to apply to was the end of the week. My mother pleaded for longer, said that this serious of a choice required research, diligence, and patience. Dad was having none of it. He knew that if he wasn't directly involved in some way, I'd use my mom's kindness against her and string her along for as long as possible.

My mom, who taught locally at a well-regarded, all-girl liberal arts school, had plenty of connections. More than once she mentioned the partnership her school had with another prestigious liberal arts school nearby. These were the types of places where the academic departments were bigger, and better known, than the athletic teams. I didn't want the small class sizes, individualized academic attention, and support that they offered. I wanted large halls full of students, a place where I could fall through the cracks, get lost, stay off the radar, and leave with something tangible that required minimal effort.

Because of my lack of ambition, I needed to conduct some of my own research. I needed to rid myself of arbitrary rankings and affordability charts and find my own set of parameters that I could get mildly excited about.

The only thing that interested me and seemed plausible as a course of study was computers—more specifically, web or video game design. But with parents who envisioned a liberal arts degree as a springboard to law or medical school, that would be a tough sell. I decided to mask my real intent under the misleading title of *computer science.*

By the end of the day I had a list of schools all across the country that offered web design and/or video game design as majors. At first I thought the list would be minimal, but my Internet ended up quitting unexpectedly because of all the open tabs. In any event, I had a direction now; at least I could look to these schools as places where I could possibly design the next bestselling video game or get to work on cutting-edge software and apply it to creating bold new webpage designs for cool companies, companies that I believed in. At the very least I'd be avoiding a minimum wage job.

I was getting ahead of myself, though. I knew I had to shorten the list and the only way that made sense to me was to do it by school mascot and colors. Looking at the computer screen, packed with data, the only thing that seemed to stand out was the mascots. This led me to a side research project. Why, and how, did a school go about choosing its mascot and colors? Hundreds of millions of dollars in endowments and a silly animal in an angry, menacing pose was the face of the institution? It didn't make sense to me but nothing about this process did.

My dad said he'd only pay for ten school applications. It was his way of keeping some semblance of control over this situation.

I had two days left and a list of almost fifty schools. Some were easier to cross off the list than they were to put on initially. I decided that any mascot that, in any form, was used to represent more than a few dozen schools was far too commonplace for me. Also, the colors would play a significant role. If I was going to commit myself to this and move to a college town, then I might as well be able to go somewhere where the streets weren't lined with ugly banners consisting of traditional, bland colors. Any type of religious mascot was out of the question as well. Something about a Saint or a Friar just didn't get me excited to be a part of that college.

My list turned out to be twelve, not ten. I was proud that I'd come this far, reached my goal, and narrowed down the choices so that I would be able to present my parents with a list that represented my future.

My list consisted of Buckeyes and Beavers, Banana Slugs and Blue Hens, Ducks and Gamecocks, Wolverines and Badgers, Fighting Irish and Cardinals, Tar Heels and Horned Frogs.

I secretly placed the schools into three categories. One was full of schools that I had no chance of getting into. Another represented schools with the best athletic departments. The final category was for the mascots, the furry little crowd-pleasers as I dubbed them. I ranked each list one to twelve and then averaged out the scores to come up with the rankings.

Based on my quick calculations, I knew that Notre Dame, North Carolina, and Stanford, while high on my list (Notre Dame because of a leprechaun, North Carolina because it had its own shade of blue, and Stanford because it had the audacity to use a tree as a mascot), presented the biggest problems academically. In fact, the only schools that I felt I could get into without a problem were Delaware and UC Santa Cruz. Both had major positives and drawbacks. If I went out to the West Coast, I'd be as far away from my parents as possible, able to enjoy the sun and the sand, and proud that my school might have the most original mascot in the country. But the sports there weren't nationally known and I doubted whether I was the California type. Delaware, on the other hand, had a great video game design program, a good mascot, and a recent graduate who was now a starting quarterback in the NFL. But it was much closer, maybe too close. I could already envision my mother dragging my father along for a long weekend under the guise of wanting to see the campus and checking out a football game.

Oregon State had weather that I was most used to, and Oregon's colors, mascot, and recent success in football were making it more and more attractive. The other schools were no duds either, as they seemed to have the right combination of school size, massive athletic departments, nationally ranked teams, and cool and unusual mascots.

This was not going to be an easy choice. It was going to be an even harder sell to my parents. I even had a day to spare, which gave me a chance to prepare my arguments. I knew that from an outside perspective, this list would seem completely illogical and haphazardly put together. The list also could crush my mom once she realized that I could be anywhere from several states away to clear across the country—the final dagger in what was already a tumultuous relationship. Dad would want figures, the money, the bottom line as to how much it was going to cost him to give me that final push out into adulthood.

That night, after having trouble falling asleep, I began to dream of a commercial that I had recently seen while watching a college football game. It was the one where the mascots of a certain conference went away to summer camp and competed against one another. I think it was for Capital One, but that wasn't important. The mascots looked alive, bursting at the seams with fun and exuberance. They were like the adult version of Disney characters, allowing me to project all of my childlike immaturity onto them.

I woke up to the smell of freshly baked blueberry muffins. Mom usually saved her muffins for special occasions like birthdays and Christmas morning. It was her last-second attempt at trying to coax me into choosing a school nearby.

Dad was sitting at the kitchen table, hunched over a cup of hot coffee, the vapors rising up into the air around him. He was making a show of not eating the muffins, proving some subtle point that had become routine during their almost thirty years of marriage.

"Good morning sweetie. How'd you sleep? I made you some muffins. I was thinking maybe we could go and rent a few movies today and just take it easy."

Dad grumbled to himself, "Rent? He steals them for free off the Internet all day. Where's your list?"

"Oh why don't you relax? He just woke up. There'll be plenty of time for that."

"Let me see it," he said.

I slid the piece of paper across the table, confident that my chosen mascots would give me the courage to prevail over his logical and rigid mindset.

Dad studied the list, making snide remarks as he made his way down it. After a few minutes he handed it to Mom, who was still chipper with anticipation and brimming with hope. Her face fell within seconds, dropping the paper to the ground once she realized that this was happening, that her baby was willing to get as far away as possible from her to get his education. She seemed to take it personally, like the list was a direct condemnation of her mothering abilities.

"Some fine schools…on this list," she said, her throat heavy with suppressed feelings. "A few standouts compared to the others, but…well, how did you come up with these schools in particular?"

Dad said, "The why isn't important, dear. Can't you just appreciate the end result and not worry about the process?"

"It's just a big decision. I want to make sure he's fully considered all of his options. I don't want him to get his hopes up and then…"

"Then what?" I finally spoke up.

"I just want to make sure you're not setting yourself up for disappointment, honey," she said.

"Stop babying him, will you? Nothing's for sure. There's only one way to find out if he's good enough and that's to send out the applications and wait." He got up from the table, swallowed his coffee in one gulp, and shuffled into the living room.

I looked over at my mom furiously scrubbing an already clean pan. She was at an angle with her back mostly facing me but I could see over her right shoulder slightly. Her hair was tucked behind her ear, exposing her cheek and jawline. The early morning sun was coming through the window, shining brightly on her face, revealing her weathered features. Wrinkles—deep, hard, and pronounced—had taken shape around her eyes and were fighting for control of most of her face. I don't know when this happened. It was hard to put a specific date on the aging process. It was the first time in a long, long while that I actually looked at her, studied the contours of her face. I wanted to get up and go to her side, reassure her somehow, tell her that everything would work itself out. But I couldn't, because I had my own still-unanswered questions running through my head.

She glanced back at me momentarily, as if she could feel the weight of my eyes on her. Her eyes were clouded with tears. I instantly looked away, as if caught looking at something for a moment too long. My eyes locked onto my list on the table. I couldn't stand to see her so vulnerable. I waited for her to continue cleaning, quickly left the kitchen, and went up to my room.

I remained in my room for the rest of the day. The house was silent. I looked out my window a few times just to make sure that their cars were still in the driveway. My attention turned to the back of my mom's car. She always backed into the driveway, scared of having to back into the main road from our gravel drive. Decals littered her bumper and spilled over to her back windshield. Most of them were oddly shaped artifacts of my parents' combined academic triumphs. If you didn't know us you'd assume we were a larger family.

It was an old car, the first they bought together as husband and wife. Mom used it to go back and forth from the college, putting just enough miles on it to make it worth getting a new transmission.

I could still make out the outline of the only decal that I contributed. It was a few years ago, right after high school. I decided it'd be funny to make light of my current academic status. It was really just a gag sticker, given for free as a thank you for buying a certain amount of video games online. It read "School of Hard Knocks" and underneath that was the tagline, "Proud Recipient of a Good Enough Diploma."

Mom went crazy when she saw it, yelps of disappointment coming from her mouth as she stormed up the stairs to my room. My dad was more upset that I had chosen to replace their Clinton '92 sticker with this one: "What the hell is wrong with you? What are you turning into, some right-wing lunatic?"

I assured him it wasn't a political statement, saying, "It was just a joke guys. I mean, to be honest, I was drunk. Sorry."

Mom said, "Oh great, now you're an underage drinker?"

"I'd rather have him be a drunk than a conservative," Dad responded.

My mother refused to help me with my applications, not wanting any part in the process that would have me moving far away from her. I applied for early admission since it was the off-season for applications and my dad didn't want me to wait. I didn't need my high school transcripts, thank God, because I'd dropped out and got my GED. I still needed proof of my passing the exam. I figured my mom still had the piece of paper that officially declared me a high school graduate because she was the one who took care of most of the paperwork in the house. Bills, greeting cards, all of that stuff that my dad couldn't be bothered with—he just sort of silently left it up to my mom, quietly thankful that she was the type of person who liked to organize things.

I found the diploma in a drawer in the kitchen, tucked in with long-forgotten takeout menus from the local Chinese and Italian restaurants. I tore through the drawer, furiously trying to find some other piece of paper, some semblance of evidence that this wasn't just a space for forgotten items. All I found were pocket calendars that hadn't been used in a few years and a pile of business cards with my mom's old job title listed.

I was on my own in this thing. My father was providing the capital but there'd be no emotional support. From that day forward, I realized that this whole college experiment, me moving out and starting on my own, was something I wanted, even needed. I had outgrown this house, this life, and my childhood. It was a dead end road. That much had become clear.

I spent the next few weeks at the local library, determined to write the perfect admissions essay. My paper needed to be exceptional if I was going to have any chance at getting into the majority of the schools I chose. Not content with my first draft, I went back and fudged the truth of my circumstances. I played up certain events and made up other hardships in the hopes that I would be viewed as a project, a person in need of help—someone who, despite the many obstacles he faced, overcame them and was ready to take on the next chapter of his life.

It sounded good. The narrative I'd created, as I went back and continued to edit the essay, started to become my own. Slowly, I was becoming the person I was writing about. I had morphed myself into this fragmented person, thirsty for the next level of education, for a true learning and life experience. By the end I didn't feel guilty over what I'd done. In fact I began to sense that I deserved to be admitted to these places based solely on my creativity, my resourcefulness, and my ability to transform my otherwise dull, underachieving suburban upbringing into something worthy of attention from a panel of admission counselors.

I figured I could get into a few schools and have a choice of where to go. My essay had given me confidence and my new identity provided me with a sense of comfort. As I sent off the applications, I felt assured that it was only a matter of time until I could leave home for a new, more exciting life.

By this time my feelings had changed considerably. I had gone from thinking of school as a more attractive option than real work to considering it more of a necessity. I needed school to prove to my father that I was a man, capable of standing on my own two feet. School would also provide me the chance to prove myself intellectually to my mom. This wasn't just about me doing something with my life. This was my chance at redefining my role in the family. I could now be something more than the disappointment, the one who never lived up to expectations.

Waiting turned to boredom quickly. Six to eight weeks turned into three months. I called admissions offices only to be put on hold or redirected to someone who had less of an idea as to what I was talking about than the previous person. My emails went unanswered. I had gone from being completely dependent on my parents to reliant on a faceless group of strangers in a boardroom in some university building high atop a hill.

Things had become tense around the house. Dad started working longer hours, staying at the office until eight or nine at night so he wouldn't have to deal directly with us at the dinner table. Mom, unable to completely lose herself in her work and disassociate like Dad, took her pain out on herself. The clothes remained dirty, piling up in the laundry room, slowly reaching knee-high level. The sink was full of dirty dishes, despite her heavy reliance on takeout since my decision to leave for school. She even began to take Fridays or Mondays off from work, giving her an extended weekend of moping around the house in her bathrobe and slippers.

I spent my days differently than before. I stayed away from video games and porn. I chose to make my presence known. It was my last-ditch effort at going out on my own terms. It would've been easier on all of us, most notably my mom, if I just stayed in my room and let the days quietly drift away until I heard back from the schools. Instead, I made up for her inaction by cooking my own meals. I made a mess of the kitchen and spent my pot money on daily trips to the health foods market. If this was to be my last time at the house, I wanted it to be memorable, more for my mom's sake than anything else. I hoped that her final memory of me living at home would be positive. I was trying to mature and I wanted her to notice. A part of me was still tied to my childlike need for her approval.

Just as I had molded myself for the college essays, I shaped my new being out of a need to replace the only life that I knew. I wasn't just going towards college and adulthood; I was leaving my childhood behind.

The first school that responded was Stanford. It was a small envelope with my name and address printed unevenly, the result of a typewriter. As I ran the envelope across my fingertips, an image of some admissions office secretary, busily pounding away at an ancient typewriter one envelope at a time, formed in my head.

I wasn't entirely surprised by the contents of the mail. It was brief and impersonal, bordering on the verge of indifferent detachment with an air of condescension. If I were honest with myself, I'd admit that I wasn't expecting to be admitted. It was a long shot at best. A Hail Mary tossed by a mediocre student in the hopes of getting as far away as possible from this house, this boring existence.

Dad took the news in stride, not allowing himself to even entertain the idea of me living off of them a moment longer. Mom hid her excitement. She needed to deceive herself, paint a portrait where she was only a day's drive away from me, allowing her to continue to play the role of the dutiful, caregiving mother. She still held close the notion of my going to a school nearby, choosing Delaware if need be or, better yet, giving in to her silent, passive-aggressive behavior and choosing a school of her liking.

I expected the rejection letters to begin pouring in after Stanford. But a funny thing happened. Nothing. For weeks. And as the weeks turned to months, my dad's only solution was to blame me, offering, "You probably screwed up the mailing address or something." My mom realized that the longer they waited, the better the chance that I got accepted. Sure, each school was different, but certain universal truths held pat regardless of the school. The bigger the envelope, the better the news. So I waited, giving up all the power to these faceless institutions onto which I projected my wildest dreams of independence.

Parcels came and went. Mass mailings promised opulent grand prizes like all-inclusive paid cruises to the Caribbean. Mom was hopeful, Dad always threw them away before they made it to the kitchen table. I suspect this was at the heart of many of their problems. Her relentless positivity clashed against his never-ending pessimism. Optimism and pragmatism made strange bedfellows. Each new day marked itself as the one that would possibly turn our well-rehearsed trio into a combative, grumpy duo.

With each slim envelope arriving at our doorstep, my mom's mood seemed to lift. Now it was Dad's turn to sulk about my future, albeit for a completely different reason. He stayed up nights, long after work, dinner, and Mom going to sleep, hunched over the PC in his library. The only thing lit was the screen bouncing back to illuminate his squinted eyes.

I caught him in one of these all-night marathon sessions. I wanted to remain unnoticed, to be a fly on the wall, a silent observer to his quirkiness. But after a few minutes of watching, I noticed something in him. I noticed a previous version of myself, pensive and obsessive. I cracked the door open slowly, allowing the creaking of our old house to take over and make my arrival known.

"Hey buddy, what are you doing up so late?" he asked.

"I could ask you the same thing."

"Just doing a bit of research."

"Work related?" I wanted to catch him in the act.

"Not exactly."

"Well?"

"I logged in and found a window open for the local community college. Your mother was the last one to use the computer and I'm wondering what she's up to."

"I'm sure there's a reasonable explanation for it. Have you asked her?"

"No, if I confront her, it'll turn into a fight. You know how defensive she gets."

"So what are you going to do?" I asked.

"I'm reading her emails."

"What?"

"You heard me. Don't act so shocked. Besides, I'm just looking for certain information."

"That doesn't matter. What you're doing is completely wrong," I said with an air of defiance.

"Grow up already, will you. Besides, I doubt you'll be on her side for much longer. Take a look at what I found."

As I leaned in to look at the screen I wondered if he did the same with my email.

"How did you get into her email?"

"Her password is Henry1985. Precious, isn't it?" he said with a smirk.

I focused on the screen and found several emails from my mom's school account, sent to the three closest community colleges. They were formal in tone, and she made sure that her academic standing and position were well known. It also showed her motherly side, as she had stated that I was ill equipped to go out on my own. She continued her scheme by dangling obscure promises if she were to get her way. Being in her position, she said, gave her some clout amongst her colleagues at her school. She even floated the idea of a pipeline program that would streamline the process of transferring students graduating from those community colleges. A win-win situation, as she put it.

I was angry and confused. I wanted to confront her, to ask why she couldn't support me and adjust her expectations of me to match my goals.

"So now what?" I asked.

"Don't worry, I'm taking care of everything as we speak. Go to bed, this isn't any of your concern. Besides, this would all be a moot point once you get an acceptance letter, right?"

"Right, goodnight."

I can't say that I felt guilty about my impending departure. It was really only a matter of time before my parents would split up. Their divorce was almost inevitable and I'd often wondered whether they were staying together for my sake. Of course they'd never admit that to me. That type of honesty wasn't an abundant quantity in our house.

By the time the second package arrived, I had completely quit smoking pot and limited my video game use to less than an hour a day. I channeled my anger towards my mom by cleansing myself, letting the frustration slide off rather than overwhelm me. I felt that if I somehow gave up my most cherished possessions and activities, then I would deserve something good to happen to me. It was my feeble attempt at undoing years of underachieving. All I could do was hope that the words "promise" and "potential" were still tossed around admissions offices, that they still held the same weight. I didn't care how I got in, I just needed the door open for a moment. Then, I promised myself, I would take advantage of the opportunity.

Notre Dame sent a similar package to the one that Stanford had mailed a while back. This time, their logo, the Fighting Irish, was on the top corner of the envelope. It seemed more official and even the letter itself was longer and a bit more personal. They loved my essay but couldn't look past my grades. Because I had dropped out and had never taken my SAT, I had to show my GED scores. My test score was high, in the top 10% nationally for that year, but not high enough to allow an institution of their caliber to grant me admission.

Mom looked over the letter and after a moment of nodding her head in agreement said, "They might be onto something, honey. After all, you don't present a strong case for admissions. Certainly an intriguing one, but far from a shoe-in, to be sure."

I sulked back to my room. Before I shut my door, I could hear my mom, still not finished with her friendly advice. "I'm sorry, it's just the truth. You'll be fine, you just have to find a school that appreciates your unique talents. You know there's a school out there for everyone."

I slammed the door closed, locked it, and reached for the last of my pot. I opened the bag and toyed with the bud, bringing it to my nose and smelling it, letting its aroma overcome the echoes of my mom's words. I fell asleep without smoking.

Dad was standing over me the next morning. I didn't know how long he had been watching me.

"How did you get in?"

"You think I don't have a key to every room in this house? If you can lock it, I can unlock it."

"What time is it?" I asked.

"Almost noon. I wanted to make sure you weren't going to just sleep the day away because of the rejection."

"Not anymore, no."

"Well, there's more. I wanted to ask you if you had any backup plans. You know, just in case you don't get into any of the schools you applied to?"

"Do we have to get into this already. I'm only zero for two, give it some time," I said.

"We're just concerned, that's all."

"We, or you?"

"Don't start with that again," he said.

"Why does it feel as though I've already lost?"

"You haven't lost already. What are you talking about? With that type of attitude, how are you going to even make it through school if you can't handle a few rejections?"

Dad rubbed his forehead and squinted, looking down at my stained carpet. "Remember what I told you about keeping our conversation between you and me. Lunch is ready and the games start in a bit," he said.

I had programmed my television to tune into the games involving the schools that I had applied to. It was a fall Saturday afternoon and that meant college football, something that my father and I had bonded over since I was a young boy.

Piles of snacks and liters of sodas were stacked on the coffee table in the living room. Mom, never the sporting type, was in the library reading a book. This was going to be a day for my dad and me.

Michigan was playing Ohio State. The game was being played in Columbus, Ohio. It hadn't started yet and the announcers were perched high above the field in their press box with their backs to the field. They pinpointed the keys to victory and highlighted All-American players. They talked of teenagers like they were professionals and discussed the national championship implications. Most of all, however, they went over the rivalry. Words like *honor* and *tradition* were thrown around without a second thought.

Just before kickoff, the lead announcer narrated a highlight clip that showcased all of the important moments in the game's history. It began with grainy footage of a mud-soaked field, both teams wearing different shades of black. Leather helmets dominated the first half of the highlight before giving way to colored artifacts of the game. Maize and blue clashed against scarlet and gray, showing long-dead stars of the gridiron as they fought for bragging rights.

Being from Maine, we never had a real, true college football team on the national level. Of course the state university had a decent team, but it never played for a national championship because it was in a different, smaller division. Besides, we were more of a hockey state than anything else. We stuck to the nationally recognized programs. Dad never had one single favorite team. He was a sucker for superstars. The legend of LSU's Billy Cannon captured my dad's fascination as a young boy. Roger Staubach showing the world that the academies still had superior athletes brought him to the edge of his seat every time Navy aired. Archie Griffin's mid-70s dominance with back-to-back Heisman Trophies gave my dad a blueprint for how to play the running back position when he was a young man.

He liked over-the-top personalities, those certain few who could rise above the game and enthrall an entire country, breaking through the boundaries of the game and coming out above the fray as more than simple athletes. He liked the icons; the religious zealotry that these players were followed with excited him. Around the time I was born, when he was glued to the television every Saturday autumn afternoon, he followed players like Marcus Allen, Herschel Walker, Doug Flutie, and Bo Jackson. Most recently we shared an affinity for Tim Tebow, Cam Newton, and Robert Griffin III. It was something we shared, and no matter how much I grew up and began to break free from the constraints set by my old man, it was hard not to return to our living room every September for the next four months' worth of Saturdays.

As Michigan took the field, a chorus of jeers and boos rained down on them from the crowd of over 100,000 people. A moment later, led by the scarlet flag bearing a gray "O," Ohio State rumbled out of the locker room and the camera began to shake. The band, Brutus the Buckeye, the cheerleaders, the hordes of uniformed young men jumping up and down as they huddled closely together in preparation for a common goal—it all got to me. The emotion and electricity that came from the student section, jumping in unison to music with bass that rumbled the core of the stadium, never got old. In this tiny pocket of the Midwest, on this Saturday afternoon, tens of thousands of people were openly worshipping at the altar of college football. The hair on my neck stood upright and my dad put his beer down and moved up in his seat like a child trying to get a better view of a Disney movie.

Just before kickoff Dad let his guard down, allowed himself to not be a superfan for a moment, and asked me a question.

"So, who 'ya got in the game?"

He knew that I had applied to both. This was his way of talking about my future.

"Tough choice. Ohio State is at home so that's gotta be worth something. I'm gonna go with Michigan though."

"Why?"

"Shoelace," a reference to the Michigan quarterback Denard Robinson and his penchant for wearing his cleats unlaced.

"Braxton Miller ain't too bad of a quarterback himself," my dad said.

"True, but he looks like he's thirty."

We didn't speak again until halftime. It was the perfect afternoon. The game kept us entertained. At the end of the first quarter the score was tied at 14. Sometime during that first quarter, I can't recall when, I had fallen into a trance. I felt stoned, but in a more controlled sense. Everything about the game was perfect. The horns from the band section boomed beautifully across the artificial turf field, the rafters shook as students and alumni swayed along to the upbeat anthems projected through the loudspeakers. For the first time in a long time, I felt that I was part of something bigger and less complicated. There was going to be a winner and a loser and there were rules. Everything was clear-cut, in black and white. Even if my team lost, I knew that they would play again next year, just like the teams from previous generations had. This giddiness, this comfort, was what I had been searching for all along.

Ohio State pulled away in the third quarter and by the fourth quarter the stadium had turned into one large party. Students were crowd surfing; the band had dotted the "I" at halftime. All seemed well. For those three hours, on that campus in Middle America, nothing was wrong with the world. To be honest, it didn't even matter who won. It was the act, participating in my small way, that made the day memorable. Wearing my lucky shirt and sweat-pants, crossing my fingers for good luck before field goal attempts—it was my entire simple, if feeble, role.

By the end of the game, my need to go away to school had been finalized. It was more than just getting out of my hometown and avoiding getting a real job. This was about being a part of a larger community of my choice. My dad always said you couldn't choose your family but you could tell a lot about a man by the company he kept. I wanted to be surrounded by these people who had passion. If all of these people could surround one stadium and coalesce around one cause and one college, then there were surely more similar opportunities out there, at every campus across the country.

I needed to explore, to tap into that energy and use it to better myself. To harness the tradition, history, and nostalgia of all of these great football programs into something that I could claim for myself. As the final whistle blew, I felt confident that come next fall, as Dad watched his games, I would be one of many in a crowd, somewhere out there experiencing the thrills and disappointments, the ecstasy and agony, the semi-religious quality of college football. If that couldn't get me excited for college, then nothing could.

I was mowing the lawn when the mailman came by a few days later. He came out of his toy-like car with a large pile of mail bundled together with a rubber band. This was it. I met him on the walkway leading to our door. I needed to be the first one to touch the letters. Somewhere in that pile represented my future for the next four years.

I came inside and put the mail on the kitchen table. The thump from the weight of it startled my mom, who was washing the dishes. She turned to face me, looking me directly in the eye as if she didn't want to acknowledge the mail on the table. I wasn't sure how many of them there were and neither was she. We both knew that it was enough to get me out of this place.

I counted nine in total, making the combined number stand at eleven. If an acceptance wasn't somewhere in this pile, then I only had one last, fleeting chance. I rifled through the heap, desperately searching for a larger package. There was none. Sitting down, bracing for the worst, I let my mom open them.

As she read aloud in her perfect diction, my heart sank a little lower. She read every word slowly and loudly, causing my father to enter the room and sit beside me. Each one read like the previous one. "While you're a very attractive candidate, we're sorry to inform you that we cannot, at this time, accept your application for admission." My father scoffed after each negative declaration. But my mom continued on, reading every word, every fake compliment, every empty promise of applying next year, every statistical assertion that it was, in fact, a numbers game and not to take it personally.

But I did take it personally. How could I not? A bunch of faceless institutions had deemed me unworthy of paying them to go there. Whatever sense of self-confidence I had was gone. I felt an empty pain in the pit of my stomach start to form. It was like a balloon full of glass shards—

unable to break through but never-ending, always growing outward, ever expanding.

I touched each letter, after my mom had finished reading it, as if feeling for some hidden clue. I let my fingers slowly roll over the slightly raised lettering on the expensive office paper. When she finished with the final letter, she sat down next to me. There were no words to say because all she had were empty ones. She sat in silence, hoping that Dad or I would take the lead and speak up, navigate our next collective course of action.

"You still got one more kid. Just hope that Oregon sees something in you that you didn't know you had," my dad said before he got up and left.

Mom waited until Dad left the room before speaking.

"It's not the end of the world, honey. We'll figure something out."

"What does that even mean?" I asked.

"I just don't want to see you get depressed because of all of this. You still have plenty of options."

"Yeah right," I scoffed.

"What's that supposed to mean?"

"Nothing, I'll see you in the morning."

"Henry, no matter what, we'll figure something out that works for all of us. Okay? I don't want you to worry."

She stood there at the base of the steps, smiling as I climbed the staircase to my bedroom.

When the final piece of mail arrived, our house was at a turning point. Dad hadn't admitted to hacking into Mom's email account and she didn't know yet just how close she was to being uncovered. I just sat patiently in the background, hoping to be a Duck.

The letter was small, like the others. Mom's words were the same, but this time spoken with a more chipper inflection, as if each word, each phrase building towards the inevitable "No thank you, you're not good enough for us," couldn't come out of her lips soon enough.

Halfway through I asked her to stop. She continued. I screamed at her to stop. She continued, this time reading faster, trying to get to the end. I got up and ripped it from her hands and tore it up.

"You happy now?"

"Why would I be happy?" she asked.

"I know, we know…everything."

I looked to Dad who in turn looked to Mom, creating a triangle of momentary quiet anxiety.

"What is he talking about?" my mom asked.

My dad looked back to me, eyes darting back and forth between each of mine, looking for directions.

"I'm talking to you!" she screamed.

"Stop being so dramatic. Sit down," he said.

"Dad found your emails, you know, your whole plan for what to do with me."

"What? I'd hardly put it that way. I just thought a two-year degree might be good for you. Then you could reapply and finish up at one of these schools," she said before turning to Dad. "How could you invade my privacy like that?"

"Your privacy? What about his? Our boy isn't your little puppet. He's not even your little Henry anymore. He's grown up. It's time you let him go!"

"Funny you giving advice. How convenient that would be, wouldn't it. You just want him out of the house for good. This whole independence spiel is nothing more than your way of throwing money at a perceived problem," she said, mascara running down her cheeks.

"Oh come off it. This isn't about us! What are we going to do with him now?"

Dad's words rang through the room. He looked shocked. Amazed at himself for the momentary outburst. There was nothing left to say. No words could take back the look of regret and anger in his eyes and the guilt and embarrassment in hers.

I headed to my room, the only sound coming from the grandfather clock ticking loudly in the corner.

A few hours later the two started up again. Free from my presence, they spoke with little restraint.

"You've got to let him go, Nina. This isn't healthy!"

"What do you know about healthy? You don't care where he goes as long as he goes. This isn't a business decision."

"There's no reasoning with you," he said.

"What's the harm in splitting the difference? He'll still go to school but he can commute and live here."

"Why, so you can smother him for a few more years?"

"You asshole, don't make this about me. Don't try and turn me into some kind of overbearing mother. Besides, there are worse things," she said.

"I'm not doing this. I refuse to get into a competition to see which one of us is the better parent. It's sick and no one wins."

"It's not a competition. It's called love, Jim," she said.

"Look, either he goes or I do. And I won't be coming back. We can't enable him for the rest of his life!"

I ran down the hallway and skipped down the stairs, trying to interject before some final outburst ended everything. I was too late. At the bottom step my mom spoke up in a calm voice.

"The fact that you're giving me this ultimatum shows how little you care, how warped your thinking is. I choose Henry, I choose him because he didn't ask for this, I choose him because I made him, I choose him because you've changed so much in the past few years, you've become emotionless, a fraction of the man I fell in love with."

"Mom, stop!" I yelled.

"Get out and don't come back," she said.

Dad turned to me. Looked me up and down slowly before speaking.

"Good luck with all this kid."

His eyes were red and misty but no tears came out.

Mom was sobbing. She was feeling for the three of us. I wanted to hug her, to keep her safe and somehow unworry her about the future, but I couldn't. I was scared too. Scared to stay, scared to go, scared to see the family ripped apart over my indecisiveness.

Dad left the next day. He only had a duffel bag's worth of stuff with him. He said he would come back for his things on the weekend. It started the following weekend, bright and early; Dad began emptying our house of half of its belongings, one piece at a time. Mom would sit and watch, deliberately taking notes of what he was taking. She refused to give an inch, to give up anything she deemed hers. They fought for hours over used books and antiques. It seemed childish, but at the same time therapeutic. I stayed in my room, door cracked open just enough to hear the whole thing.

In the ensuing weeks, Mom began to order things to fill the house. Catalogs from Restoration Hardware and Crate & Barrel were strewn about the living room. Samples of colors and textures were laid across her bed. It was my mom's thinly veiled attempt at filling the cold empty space on my dad's side of the mattress.

I remained quiet, letting her do what she needed to do. The irony of the whole thing wasn't lost on me. She was spending money on knickknacks to help her fill the emotional emptiness directly caused by her not wanting me to go away to college and stay local, which in turn had also freed her from having to spend an obscene amount of money on my tuition.

Within two months of Dad's departure, the house was fuller than when he took the final box of his belongings with him. The FedEx deliveryman became such a commonplace thing that Mom had even begun to flirt with him, inviting him in for coffee and sweets. He always said no, thank you, that he had more deliveries to make, but I suspect my mom wasn't worried about the results. It seemed to be more of an exercise to her. To see if she still held some appeal.

It had become too much—the drama, the daily affirmations my mother would say aloud to herself in the bathroom, the materialism, the retail therapy—all of it was just too much for me to even care about anymore. My opinions had slowly withered away to a dull nothingness that seemed to affect everything else in my daily life.

I took control of Dad's study, carving out a space for myself other than my cramped, pot-smelling room in the top corner of the house. I needed that room, needed the smell that still remained from his things that had been removed. The lethargy, the hangover from the past few months still weighed on me deeply. I used the room as more of a place to hide, knowing full well that my mom refused to set foot in the room out of some silent protest or principle. It was my safe haven, my adult version of a childhood fort.

Slowly I filled the empty shelves with my own books, bought from the sale bin at the local library or stolen from the Barnes & Noble at the nearby mall. I kept the remnants of my former life, that of underachievement and slacking, upstairs in my bedroom. Dad's old study was devoid of any video games or television. The only transplant was my computer. I pirated copies of various design applications and Microsoft Office. Then I downloaded an application that blocked the Internet and removed all of my bookmarks.

I began to replicate the persona that I had created in my application essays. Applying myself for the first time in my life, I found the life that I had fabricated and embellished in those essays hard to live up to, but it served as a good distraction from my surroundings.

I closed down my world, blacked out everything around me. My world became smaller, more intense. Mom hovered around me, not quite willing to broach the subject of school yet. She knew that the scabs of what she had done and what Dad had said were still fresh. But I was waiting for the conversation to be brought up, and I wasn't going to be the one who did it.

I was doing things incrementally but I was making progress. I taught myself Photoshop and some basic web design. I began writing a daily journal; it was something in which to record my feelings. I still didn't see a clear path, from where I was, that led out of the house. I was trying to find my way, and for the time being, that was enough.

Dad had moved from a hotel just off the interstate into a cramped studio apartment downtown by the school. I didn't want to visit him. It was my mom who had suggested going.

"I don't want what happened between me and your father to affect your relationship with him."

I suspected that she just wanted to get a read on how he was doing.

Something about my situation with my father held the key to my future. I knew our relationship was broken and superficial. I'd have to find a way to forgive him if I wanted to move on.

The crowd on the bus grew younger as it made its way downtown. The neighborhoods were less clearly defined and separated than out in the suburbs. Sorority row was next to old eastern European immigrant communities that had been set up almost a century before.

Dad's stop was two before the main college drop-off, but still on the outskirts of campus. The address was a large but dilapidated Victorian house that had an expansive wrap-around porch. It was three stories high, with faded, chipped paint. The steps leading up to the front door were uneven and the mailbox was half the size of the front door. I quickly skimmed through the names, not quite sure if my dad had entrenched himself enough yet to put his name on this place. I didn't find his name. It had every other conceivable name on it though. Residents with names like "PLANT MAN" and "FRISBEE" could be rubbed off with a little work to expose another name entirely. It was at this moment that I felt a touch of sadness, even empathy, for Dad.

The door swung open, almost hitting me in the left shoulder. Out came a pack of guys my age. A stench of pot and menthol smoke blew by me as they skipped down the steps, out through the lawn, and to the sidewalk. I slipped inside before the door closed.

I found my dad's apartment by elimination; his door was the only one without a name stickered onto the front. He opened the door almost immediately, as if he was looking out the peephole.

"Come in," he said.

"Thanks."

I quickly scanned the place. It didn't take long. The apartment was nothing more than one room, except for the bathroom that was tucked away in the corner. The place reminded me of a set, straight from either an old television show like *The Honeymooners* or an off-Broadway play. No cabinets or closets, just a desk that served as the kitchen island and living room and dining room table. The kitchen had a mini-fridge. Right next to it were a few plates and pots and pans piled in the sink.

His mattress was on the floor with a few open boxes scattered next to it. He had a futon, which looked like it had been in the room since before I was born. More boxes lined the route to the bathroom.

He sat on the edge of the bed, knees almost up to his chin. I sat on the futon, waiting for him to start talking.

"So, what do you think?" he asked, motioning with his hands outward, almost touching both walls at the same time.

"It's cozy," I said.

"How's your mother?"

"Not well. She's been going crazy trying to fill the house with random things," I said.

Dad seemed to take joy in this last statement, although he did his best to hide his outward happiness.

"How are you? What have you been doing?"

"Reading and writing during the day. I've been playing around with some graphic design, teaching myself some applications."

"That's good. Any news on the college front?"

"No, not yet. Dad, can I ask you a question?"

"Shoot."

"What did you mean when you said, 'Good luck with all this,' right before you left?"

He got up off the bed and went to the kitchen. Back home this would've bought him a few minutes. Here he was at the sink in ten seconds, filling himself a glass of dirty, brownish water.

"You're not stupid, Henry. You knew damn well what I meant. If you need it spelled out for you at this point, then I've been giving you too much credit all these years."

"It was just a question," I said.

"Come on Henry, think about it. I'm talking about your mother, God bless her. She's going to be the downfall of you in the end if you don't get out of there and make something of yourself. I know I'm not telling you anything new."

"And what about her? Just leave Mom all by herself? No, I'm not going to just toss her aside like you did."

At this Dad got visibly angry, the vein in his forehead beginning to throb.

"You watch yourself kid. You have no idea what you're talking about. I love your mother, always have, always will. It's not as simple as you think," he said.

"Then let me ask you this. Why is it complicated for you and her but you claim it's simple when it comes to me and her?"

He turned away but realized he had nowhere to go. He couldn't outrun or escape the question no matter how much he wanted to. I watched as this man, my father, in all his intelligence and life experience, struggled to answer a basic question I had posed to him.

I got up and told him that it was good seeing him. I said I would be back soon, and left. We both knew I was lying but he let it go unchallenged. I didn't want another argument. Besides, the bus was due to come by any minute now.

I decided to enroll in school on the bus ride back home. There was no grand plan. It just seemed like the right thing to do.

I knew that my options were limited. This didn't bother me. My limitations freed me from unhealthy expectations. I could just go to school now and figure out some stuff. Hopefully grow up and become something different, greater than what my parents had expected out of me.

That's why I chose the community college. I could've gone to a nearby school, but I didn't want it to be because of my mom's connections. This was my own thing, something I carved out for myself.

The tuition was cheap and the classes small. I signed up for an extra class on top of my regular courseload just to keep me out of the house. I was going for 18 credits that first semester. I even scoured the cafeteria walls for bulletins and flyers announcing any sort of club or extra-curricular activity.

There were no football games to go to that autumn— no grand stadium with a marching band playing a historic song, rolling in through the chipped paint tunnels where decades of other student athletes had come before. There was no homecoming, no great tailgating or fraternity scene. But, in the end, I don't think that I needed all that.

We had some sports, but they lacked the grandiosity and the scale that I once yearned for. I had wanted to lose myself in something, but I found that the journey—just going to school and keeping out of the house, away from the toxicity of my parents' crumbling marriage—was enough to fill the void I had been so anxious to plug.

I even made a few friends and found myself beginning to crash on their couches during the week. But I couldn't quite escape my mom's reach. I'd stop by the house, slowly being filled back to capacity with her newly bought items, and check in on her on the weekends, not willing to cut off ties completely like Dad had.

My school's mascot was a Tiger. Our colors were orange and black and white. A few months ago I would've run away from this place, this mock campus made up of nothing more than two-story-high cement barricades spread out along a flat area with parking lots in between. As I walked to class one day, kicking along some shards of broken glass from a dropped bottle, I realized that this campus that looked and felt like a Wal-Mart, this nothing of a school, was just what I needed.

FILL ME UP

I dreaded going to the pharmacy. I had to though. I didn't have any other options. I used to have it delivered through the mail but that took too long and cost more. The return address read Kansas City. The last time, they got lost in the mail. Never showed up. I called their hotline and was on hold for almost an hour when a woman picked up. She asked me for my Social Security number, address, and date of birth multiple times before apologizing on behalf of the company and offering a new shipment free of charge. She also added that my name would be put into a sweepstakes that was drawn at the end of every month. She said it was open to employees only but that she was giving me hers. The winning draw got a $100 gift card to some chain restaurant. I wanted to be angry, to yell, but the slight Midwestern drawl twang thing she had soothed me. By the time I hung up I was apologizing to her. My meds never came and I never won any gift card and I never called the hotline again. And that's how I got mixed up with having to go to the pharmacy.

The local pharmacy was nothing more than a doctor's waiting room, bombarded with enough useless knick-knacks that if you're going to pick up medication, you almost get distracted into thinking you're healthy. Then there were the familiar faces, the former classmates, the ex-girlfriend, teachers, and parents. It was all too much for me to handle.

My dad was sick, in bed with some weird summer mutation of the flu. I walked to the CVS reluctantly, my breaths more pronounced and strained with every step further away from my door. My chest tightened, my knees grew wobbly, and my hands began to moisten with sweat. I hadn't been outside in thirteen days. There wasn't a cloud in the sky and the sun beamed down on me like it had been waiting for me.

I ran through the details of the television program from last night. Replaying certain portions of the segment, trying to replicate the correspondent's particular inflections when it came to certain words. It was the feature piece on *60 Minutes*, a show my father refused to miss no matter how sick he was. When the picture of the giant pink pill flashed as the backdrop for the introduction to the piece, I wanted to reach for the remote. To at least make an effort at switching the channel, redirecting the conversation to something else.

It was a piece aimed to educate the public but, by the end, induced more of a paranoid state of mind. My father adjusted his seat in a half-hearted attempt to drown out, or at least compete with, the voices of concern and alarm coming from the television. We remained quiet through-out, letting words like *alarming new results found* and *a possible deadly mix when combined with certain other drugs* string themselves together, echoing against the four walls of our living room.

After the show ended I left the room, not wanting to make eye contact with my father and feeling as though I'd somehow done something wrong. As this ill-placed guilt weighed me down, I took refuge in my room, locking the door behind me. There'd be no quiet moment shared watching the sunset like we usually did, just an abrupt end to the day. I could hear the television from my room as I fell asleep.

When I woke, the morning news was on. I found my father slumped over in the chair, snoring with his mouth open. I woke him up and helped him to his bed, not wanting to make a big deal over his sweaty forehead and crimson-colored cheeks.

A commercial came on, advertising a possible cash settlement for people taking the medication that I was on. It said that men who had taken the pills were more susceptible to growing breasts, and that if you were a man, then you should call and discuss a possible case against the company. I felt my chest reluctantly. A little more to grab at than when I was younger, but my weight gain could also account for it. My weight gain was directly related to my meds though. It was all interconnected, a giant row of dominoes, the first one flicked a long time ago.

Halfway towards the pharmacy, the back of my T-shirt clung to my back. Little tributaries of sweat ran idly down until they reached the top of my boxers. Cars passed by, windows open, music blaring from the speakers. Fragments of music or talk radio went whizzing by. It seemed everyone except for me was in a hurry to get somewhere.

Scott Pelley's voice rang in my ears. Words like "lethal dosage" and "Big Pharmaceutical's dark secret" pinged off the insides of my head, moving faster and gaining volume with each step. The ringing of CVS' automatic door sensor interrupted my replay of the prior night's program.

I walked down the closest aisle to the entrance, not looking up to see which one was unoccupied. I got stuck behind an old lady whose mini shopping cart seemed out of place for such a small store. I waited for her to reach for a package of mothballs before trying to make my way around her. She gave up halfway, the package one level too high, and fell back into me. I didn't stop to make sure she was fine. I was already feeling restricted, too exposed to that which I couldn't control.

My final destination was in sight in the back corner of the store. The line was about five people deep when I reached it. The font, the signs, everything became enormous. I felt as though I was being forced to read from a large print book of one-line public service announcements. "Free eye exams," "limited time only diabetic starter kits"—they all melted into one large warning. Except one.

"Please consult your pharmacist if you have any questions regarding your medication's possible side effects. Remember, it's always better to be in the know. Educate yourself to be a better patient."

I hadn't noticed the sign before. I hadn't been there in a while but wondered if they'd put it up in response to the segment on the news. The pharmacist called me up before I could formulate an answer.

"Hello, how can I help you?"

"Yeah, I just wanted to fill these prescriptions."

"Oh, of course, I just always assumed it was for your dad since he always filled them."

"Nope, no, they're for me."

I slid the papers over to him like I was passing a high school love note in class. If I could've, I would've folded it up just to make sure nobody else but him could read the medications and piece together my mental affliction by discerning my psychiatrist's awful handwriting.

"Well, let's see what we have here. Yep, just the three of them, right?"

"Yeah."

As his attention turned to the third script, for Depakote, he hesitated. His movements grew more deliberate, more timid.

"How's the medication working out for you? I don't mean to pry, it's just that I saw that special on the news last night and…well, the side effects that just came to light are pretty scary, to be honest with you."

Diarrhea, dizziness, drowsiness, hair loss, blurred vision, ringing in the ears, tremors, and weight changes may occur.

"What, Depakote? Yeah, it's fine. I mean, I have no complaints," I said.

Chest pain, bruising, bleeding, irregular heartbeat, and swelling of the hands and feet have also been reported.

"Don't mean to be a bother, it just caught my attention. You know, I have some pamphlets, literature, in the back about the medication. Tons of it just lying back there. It's a shame really that more people don't take more of a proactive approach with their medicine."

Uncontrollable eye movements and the inability to contain leg movements (akathesia) are also possible.

"Yeah, well, I've been on it for some time now so I'm pretty well adjusted to it."

On some occasions dark urine, persistent nausea, and severe abdominal pain can be expected.

The line behind me had grown and spilled back into one of the aisles. The sweat, despite the air conditioning, was beginning to spread to my forehead and back of my neck. I needed air, room, fewer eyes on me. I could feel everyone behind me staring at the back of my head, right through me to somewhere deep down inside that I wished would remain hidden to the public.

"Good to hear. Well, everything should be ready in about an hour."

Contact your doctor immediately if your depression worsens or if you have suicidal thoughts.

I nodded, took my receipt, and brushed through the crowd. Head down and ears muted to the grumbles and moans of people saying excuse me or watch it young man.

I lit a cigarette in the parking lot, baking under the sun like a cracked omelette on a frying pan. I counted the number of side effects that I'd experienced since I was prescribed Depakote. Between the report on the television and the bits of information I vaguely remembered my psychiatrist telling me years ago, I counted seven. Seven out of the twenty, or thirty-five percent, not quite a majority but enough to keep me inside the house for another two-week stretch.

REQUIEM

The fall was a surprise, a loud thump in the night. He was nothing more than dead weight and mumbled words. His hands were mangled claws. He was slouched over, half asleep. This was his first trip to the hospital. It was a two-week stay, a hint of things to come. The night before the fall we all had dinner together, the three of us; like normal. He was chain-smoking in front of the television. We shared each other's company, mouths filled with pasta.

Now we waited, anxious for the next round of tests, the results that would determine his fate. The support staff came in and out of the room, all smiles and nods. They offered food and drinks, like a BLT would bring him back. I wanted to yell, scare them away, isolate and terrify them.

He came home, not quite pronounced healthy. We didn't care. Half of him was better than nothing. We stayed by his side around the clock. We worked on shifts. Dad just retired so we were lucky. During the day I'd stay with him while Dad restocked the medicine cabinet. He had to go to the laundromat every other day to clean the soiled sheets.

We fed him, changed him, bathed him. He was embarrassed, ashamed of what his fall turned him into. Dad and I didn't mind; it was the natural cycle of things. We were methodical and silent in our help.

Dad and I replaced knickknacks with medical supplies. We were hopeful about keeping him from the inevitable. He hung on for another month, mentally sharp but physically broken.

Things went quickly. First his appetite left, then an inability to swallow. His bowel movements were the last to go.

The ambulance came at four in the morning. Twenty hours until Santa Claus slid down the chimney. We followed behind, Dad right on the bumper, afraid that if we got there even a minute later we might miss something, some important decision. But the ER was quiet, only the nightly news in the background.

For all intents and purposes, he died on Christmas. His deceased wife, my grandma, was born on the same day. Eighty-eight years ago to the day. Thoughts of them rejoining on the anniversary were nothing more than a small consolation. They were married for fifty-four years, childhood sweethearts. She was the only woman he'd ever been with. Her love was enough for his entire life. It had been sixty years since their first date, before the great war that shaped their generation.

But he didn't go on Christmas, not quite. He still had a few more days of fight in him. But that was the day when the doctors spoke of making him as comfortable as possible. They told us that it could happen any minute now. Their pragmatism was cold, just like the tiled floors beneath my feet. They took him off the machines and told us that it was time to wait, that nothing more could be done.

Husband and wife both took their last breaths around a major event. She just days before 9/11, he between Christmas and New Year's. Terror and joy mixed into a faded memory of a relationship only ended by death.

Two full days, morphine the only thing in his system. He was down to four respirations a minute. I'd sit there and count, watchful for any changes. The next five and a half days slower, one by one, as he approached his final breath.

The last twelve years without her by his side. No more home-cooked meals, a new routine. Now he wore pajamas, let his beard grow.

Her things remained untouched, the closet still full of her clothes and Frank Sinatra records. I'd begun to cut his hair and shave him in those years since she died. Somewhere along the way I became his personal barber. With each clip and each razor he'd recite jokes to me from the latest AARP magazine. I never called him on it. I let him have his glory.

Fifty straight hours at the hospital. I went home to shower off the smell of impending death. His Medicare provided an inflatable mattress. It was still preserved; I unplugged it, watched it deflate, and imagined that his lungs made the same punctured noise somewhere deep down inside him. Their king-sized bed gone. Sides picked decades ago. He never slept on her side, even after her death. Half a bed unused. He looked so small, so old and vulnerable, asleep in that big bed all alone. I turned off the lights to his room and stood in the darkness. I matched my feelings to the surroundings. I replicated his vision, lids closed shut, blankness, nothing, nowhere.

Both of them had been fighters. She was stricken with MS as a young bride. He was dealt polio as a youth. She was an immigrant, off the boat at three. He was second generation on the streets of Brooklyn. Both were tough but softened by each other.

The local taxi company knew me by name. I'd been going back and forth between the house and hospital every day. The driver, the same one each time, mumbled broken English as I tipped him, *Merry Christmas. Good Luck.*

He used to curse in Sicilian. He called me his little *sheka*, slang for donkey. Affectionate because of the accompanying smile. In English I was *potato head* to poke fun at my Irish side.

Visiting hours didn't apply to us. The nurses came in that first night, but my dad's face—the emptiness in his eyes, his tensed muscles—told them we weren't going anywhere. We'd set up camp. Round-the-clock bedside vigil, blind faith our only companion. A priest visited the room and prayed over him, offered condolences. He was given last rites which didn't seem right, somehow unfair. He never was religious. He was kicked out of Catholic school because he carved his name into the church pew. He was left-handed; the nuns beat the devil out of him. He still complained about those "nasty penguins" as he scribbled out checks with the penmanship of a doctor.

His right eye opened slightly for the last forty-eight hours. There was no eye movement, just a glimpse, a tease of a possible recovery, but nothing more. At 4:01pm, Monday, December 30, the nurse took his wrist in his hand. He was silent for a few seconds. "Yeah, he's gone," and he walked out, not another word. It was anticlimactic and surreal.

I thought I was prepared for his passing after going through my grandma's death as a teen. She had an open casket funeral. The entire town showed up. Grandpa was quiet, not wanting a big show of things. It was just like him, dignified and reserved.

I stood at the foot of the bed. My dad at his father's side, tears in his eyes. He kissed his head and held his limp hand. I stared at the lifeless eye. It stayed on me; looked through me. I gave him a kiss on the cheek. His skin was already a bit cold.

We waited for a doctor to officially pronounce him dead. She filled out paperwork, a period at the end of the sentence of his life. The man in the bed next to us yelled at his wife in Spanish. The news was on in the background. It drowned out the silence of death, engulfed the hospital room. Stock prices, weather reports, traffic jams, sports scores. Pointless daily distractions.

We went home that night. Dad and I, alone in the house, empty and cold. There was a pile of unread mail, bills addressed to him, his name in black and white. I postponed my therapy session, unable to find the right words for what had happened, for what I felt. I wasn't ready to have his death reduced to notes jotted down on a yellow legal pad by someone who had never met him.

The sun rose the next morning. Rays penetrated through the house. Smells of him were still in the walls, the furniture. His pack of cigarettes was on the kitchen table, untouched, a reminder of his eventual mortality.

Dad took care of the arrangements. He did so silently and without complaint. He was dependable as always; like father like son. He met his father's body at the cremation site. Brought him home in a box on the passenger seat. A lifelong smoker now reduced to ashes.

We arranged a funeral. It was simple and small. He wanted to be cremated, laid to rest next to his love. A woman walked through the graveyard for early morning exercise. She was on her phone; I heard my name, a conversation about me. It was an auditory hallucination induced by stress. I didn't tell my dad because he had enough on his mind. As the minister spoke, cars whizzed behind us. It served as a reminder of life's never-ending forward movement. His words were muffled by those oblivious to our loss. I dropped a cigarette in the hole at the grave as God's words hung over us. A moment of pause, silence, but this was more significant than verses from the book; this was something between the two of us. It was something to rot away into nothing alongside him.

On that first night in bed, sleep was hard to find. I was lost in my own thoughts. That opened eye at the end watched over me as I finally slept. The house was quiet now. It used to be full with the voices from *Law & Order* and westerns. Detective Lenny Briscoe was his favorite, with his one-liners and sarcasm. The coolness of John Wayne, how he always got the girl, brought out the child in him. He'd inch closer to the television set, not wanting to miss a word.

Two weeks gone and not a single tear. I felt guilty, like I didn't love him as much somehow. Dad cried every day.

It served as a reminder of my shortcomings. All I had was that vision of his opened eye and a sense of dread, a dead end, like things would never be the same ever again.

I reached the period where everything was looked at through the prism of his death. Things seemed insignificant when compared to the memory of his cold lifeless body. His death a finality that paralyzed me, froze my emotions like the cold icicles that hung from the side of the house.

THE TIES THAT BIND US

As Colin approached his brother's house, his car broke down. He would've called Jim to give him a heads up, but he didn't own a cell phone. A side effect of his life up to this point.

It was an hour's walk to the house. The driveway alone was at least a quarter-mile. Jim had told him that the house was coming along nicely, but he still didn't know what to expect.

The house popped up unexpectedly, rising up over the mature forest of oak trees that surrounded the quiet neighborhood. Even the clouds that had followed Colin on the trip here seemed intimidated and in awe of the structure's beauty, as if not wanting to disrupt it by covering it up, if only for a brief moment.

As he rang the doorbell, nervousness came over Colin. His chest became tight and he had trouble swallowing as he waited for someone to answer the door. It reminded him of when he was called on to speak at meetings. He rolled down his sleeves, covering up his newest tattoos—his attempt at assimilating to his new environment.

The details were still fuzzy. All Jim had told him was to pack a bag, that he had a job for him. That was enough for Colin. Even though he hadn't seen Jim in months, the lure of a paycheck made the two-hour trip worth it.

It didn't matter that he had disappointed Jim by walking out on a job he set up for him right after the New Year. Jim's voice was stern and fatherly. The call came as a surprise to Colin. He hadn't been in contact with anyone in the family since his last episode.

Jim's wife, Susie, answered the door after a few minutes. A smile consumed her petite face. It scared Colin—always did. The last time he saw that look he had walked into an intervention put on by his family. He stepped slowly into the house.

"Hey Colin! How are you? It's been a while. You look good."

She stepped in for a hug, having to reach up to meet Colin's upper body. He leaned down, despite Susie being almost five-eight. At six-four, 250 pounds, Colin swallowed her diminutive frame whole as they embraced. He was careful not to squeeze too hard for fear that he'd hurt her.

"Fine and you? Where's Jim?"

"He's in the kitchen. Come on in."

Colin walked down the expansive hallway towards the kitchen. It was larger than his studio apartment. Framed pictures lined the walls. His brother posing with various important politicians and celebrities. He felt like he was in a country club.

"You're late," Jim declared as he took off his glasses and put down the newspaper.

"Yeah, sorry about that, car broke down."

"You alright?"

"Yeah, no worries. It's only about a mile from here."

"I'll call AAA. So, how are things?"

"No complaints. The place looks nice."

Jim looked around as if he were examining his surroundings for the first time.

"It's coming along nicely," Jim said.

Fearing that his brother would delve into personal matters, Colin kept the conversation on topic.

"So, what's this job you have for me?"

"Well, it's complicated."

"Isn't it always," Colin chuckled nervously as he stared at his feet. His right boot had a hole in the front.

"Anyway, my guy that's overseeing the construction got caught up recently. He claims he's got another job that he has to finish first. Long story short, I need someone to kind of grab the reins and continue the work. It's really only upstairs that's left. The five bedrooms, three bathrooms, and a small game room."

"So is it just me or will I have some help?"

"Of course, I still have most of his workers. Day laborers and the sort. Don't worry though, they're pretty good. I just need someone to overlook the operation."

Colin thought about this last statement for a moment. Surely his brother could've called any number of contractors in the area. Why him? Loyalty? Guilt? As a way to keep tabs on him? He didn't have time to analyze. He needed the money.

"So any specific time constraints? What kind of budget am I dealing with?"

"All of the supplies have been taken care of already. Most of them are out back in the garage. Ideally I'd like to have it done by the end of the summer."

Colin did the math in his head. Eighteen weeks from now. That gave him two weeks per room. Difficult but not impossible.

Jim continued, "I've squared away the payments for the first contractor and his guys are being taken care of. I guess that just leaves you. What do you think?"

Colin began to get nervous again. He pictured an envelope of money and endless possibilities. A shot at some sense of freedom. A chance to get out from under his sizeable debts.

He tried to play it off coolly. After a few minutes he cleared his throat and threw out a number. He didn't want to seem desperate, but in reality they both knew he was. Jim agreed to the $40,000 for the work, plus a stipend for living expenses. Not bad for the black sheep of the family.

With most of the details taken care of, Colin relaxed a bit. He took a seat next to Jim. He looked at the fireplace. It was a substantial configuration, easily ten feet wide and five feet deep and running all the way up to the top of the twenty-foot ceiling. The brick and woodwork must've taken months to perfect. Its size was impressive. While Colin respected the effort, the closer he examined it, the more he felt that he could do better work.

His sense of self-assurance was undoubtedly spurred on by his newfound wealth. It was an uncomfortable feeling, but it sure beat the anxiety-riddled fear that he'd grown accustomed to.

"Where are the kids?"

Jim looked at Colin as if shocked.

"School."

"Oh, right, yeah they would be. Right."

"Yeah, they get big quick."

More silence.

"Which reminds me, Susie and I are actually going to be away for the summer as well. Work stuff, just got a new deal with Parmalat actually. So they want me to go over to Italy until the end of August. We're not leaving until the end of the week. So I need you to not only work on the place but watch it for me as well."

"So it's just me?" Colin cracked a slight smile.

Jim nodded. He looked as though he already regretted his decision.

Colin stayed in the guesthouse. It was right next to the garage. He felt like a spare tool that the family wanted out of the way.

His car was at the auto repair shop in town. He managed to get his bag from the backseat before they towed it. He had brought a week's worth of clothes, two books, and his toolbox. It was everything he owned.

He dreaded eating with them, but his hunger overcame his fear. They were seated at the dining room table when Colin entered. Not wanting to make eye contact, Colin stared at the two wine bottles. He tried pronouncing their names to himself but gave up after the second syllable.

Jim noticed Colin's eyes and quickly moved the bottles out of reach.

"You want some water?"

"Yeah."

He really wanted to take the bottles and hide back in the guesthouse for the rest of the night.

Susie broke the silence minutes later.

"So, Colin, what's new? How are things?"

"Not too bad, you know. It's been difficult finding steady work."

"All you have to do is show up. Reliability is everything." Jim downed another glass of wine. It was his fourth; the main course was still warm.

"Things get complicated," Colin responded.

"Well, it's good just to have you here. I'm just sorry we have to leave so soon," Jim said.

"Me too."

"I spoke to Mom and told her you were down. She might stop by next week. You know she misses you."

Colin searched for that bottle of wine. He played with the food on his plate and remained silent.

Across the table was a picture of her with Dad as a newlywed. She couldn't have been more than eighteen at the time. Dad was nineteen. Even though it was black and white, and grainy, Colin could tell she was happy. His dad took up most of the photo. Ever since Colin's dad died when he was nine, he'd heard about how he resembled him the most out of anyone in the family. They were the only males over six feet, each with the body of a defensive end. His eyes, pointy chin, and boxer's nose were all clearly hand-me-downs as well. Colin liked the similarity, not so much because it was his dad but more so for the fact that he now had a special place within the family—something to call his own.

"Well, I have to make some calls. See you in the morning?"

"Sure," Colin answered with food in his mouth.

"Honey, everything was great. I'll see you in a bit."

Jim walked out and had the phone to his ear before leaving the room. Colin kept his head down, focusing on his plate. Susie did the same. The two finished their meals in silence.

"Your brother means well. He's just worried about you," Susie said.

They were washing the dishes. Colin's calloused hands slowly succumbed to the warm water.

"Just try and be patient with him. He just wants what's best for you."

Colin closed his eyes. His hands were now soggy.

He grabbed a large bottle of water and headed outside. The sun had been absent for a few hours and the stars had blanketed the clear, dark sky.

He took out a cigarette and lit it. He only had three left. He focused on the light at the tip of the cigarette. If he tried really hard he could hear a faint crackling sound as he inhaled. He let his lungs fill with smoke until he could feel a slight burn. This was his only relief now.

Smoke exited through his nose. He felt like a dog that had escaped from his cage.

Colin woke up to an infomercial. The guy was selling a set of Japanese knives. $19.95 plus shipping would bring his misery to an end. He chose to go to the main house to eat breakfast. He didn't have the money or the patience to wait for the sweet relief of a large, cold, shiny blade across his neck.

Imported coffee and the *New York Times* were the only things being shared at the kitchen counter between Jim and Susie. Colin grabbed a cup of coffee.

"Any plans for today?" Jim asked.

"Probably go into town. Need some smokes."

"You want a ride?" Susie asked. "I need to go to the store to pick up groceries anyway."

"I'm fine."

"Here's the keys to the Benz. We'll be here."

"Need anything?" Colin asked.

If he could pick them up something, then he wouldn't feel as though he were simply mooching off of them. Maybe he had some use after all.

"Just a few things from the store," Susie said as she blindly handed him a hundred-dollar bill and a list.

People strolled about from one store to another, no real destination in mind. Leisure dominated Main Street despite it being a weekday. At every stop sign or red light Colin would get glances. Surely he was a strange sight. Paranoia filled his body. He felt out of place. He lit up his final smoke without realizing he was still in Jim's car. His brother hated the smell. Colin smirked to himself in the rearview mirror. His green eyes twinkled for a moment. It was the first time he noticed the color back in his eyes since he last drank.

The lawns were a vibrant green and the front porches looked like they'd just been painted. Each house seemed larger than the prior and everyone had a smile on his face. As if living in Harbor Village somehow brought about unconditional happiness.

He parked in front of an antique shop. A leather chair and ottoman were in the window. The price tag was

$15,000. Colin shook his head. That was more than he made the prior year. The storefront below his apartment in Albany was a Salvation Army. It cost Colin less than $300 to outfit his entire place.

The market didn't sell any Marlboro Reds, only $15 clove and herbal cigarettes. His local bodega sold smokes for $7. Taste of the good life, Colin figured, as he used the hundred for the smokes as well as Susie's groceries.

The cashier, who couldn't have been older than Jim's kids, eyed him suspiciously as he handed over the bill. She put it up against the light. Colin wished it was fake if only to inconvenience everyone for a bit. The stuck-up bitch deserved that much. A line of people outfitted from a J. Crew magazine had formed behind him, waiting impatiently.

His palms were moist as she handed him his change. He rushed out from the store with his head down. The only thing that stopped him from using the change on beer was the fact that the place only sold six-pack bottles of Blue Moon and India Pale Ale. He wanted a case of Natural Ice or Pabst Blue Ribbon.

Colin noticed the window blinds from the kitchen move as he pulled into the driveway. Jim and Susie tried to act casual when he entered.

"Here you go," Colin said as he placed the groceries on the counter.

Before they could respond he was out of the room.

The rest of the week went by in a daze for Colin. He spent his nights hiding from Jim and Susie in the guesthouse. During the day he roamed the upstairs halls, inspecting the work that he had to do. He measured the same walls dozens of times just to keep away from a potential conversation.

On Friday morning Colin found an envelope on the dresser next to his bed. Inside was $250. A note read simply, "Here's your weekly stipend. Had to take earlier flight. Talk soon."

The house was empty. Colin took the time to check out the main floor and basement.

The basement was a game room for adults. A large bar was tucked in the near corner. As Colin turned on the lights, he noticed the dark, rich oak wood of the counter. Behind the bar were mugs and glasses from every conceivable nation. Across from the bar was a wine cellar. That alone was almost as big as Colin's apartment. Next to it was a cigar room the size of a walk-in closet. Colin grabbed a nice Cuban cigar.

Pictures of Jim standing alongside President Clinton, the Prime Minister of Ireland, and Bono—shades and all—adorned the mantle over the fireplace. The sash from when Jim was the Grand Marshal of the St. Patrick's Day Parade a few years back was hung proudly over the photos. Colin hadn't been invited to the festivities. Jim had been wary of what Colin might do and had wanted nothing to ruin his big day. Framed black and white sports photos led the way to the pool table. At the far end of the room were an antique poker table and a 70-inch television.

Colin felt like he was a child again, hanging out at the rich kid's house only because of his toys.

The main floor was a bit more understated than the basement. Downstairs was definitely his brother's design; upstairs reeked of Susie's taste. A set of stairs was all that connected Jim's childhood to his new, adult life. Jim had changed from a beer-chugging college rugby player to an investment banker in his Brooks Brothers suit, but still couldn't detach himself from his past. This whole project, the construction of the new house, Colin thought, was nothing more than a way for Jim to maintain both personas. Colin laughed to himself. *At least I know who I am,* he thought to himself. The laughter ended quickly.

He stepped outside onto the back patio and lit up the cigar. Down the hill was a trail leading to the in-ground pool. Alongside it was a pool house. Colin pictured Jim's kids using it to party all night long. He wondered how much more trouble he could've gotten into as a kid if he had come from this amount of money. The answer terrified him.

RUN

Monster, mother. Different sides of the same coin really. Her breath reeked of gin and tonic, her eyes were a watery red, and her fingers were blackened from cigarettes. She scared me. It wasn't anything in particular but rather a combination of a bunch of little things. Our conversations were one-sided and usually involved yelling, cursing, or both.

The clearest memory of my childhood was her hands. Small, pale, and freckled, her hands would tremble every morning before she had her first drink. One to steady the shakes, two to get to baseline, and the rest to forget about everything else. Whenever we were in public I had to make sure that she had a little bottle stashed away in her purse so that she could keep herself leveled. That was what she liked to call it, getting leveled. She figured if she made it sound innocent, then she wasn't really guilty of doing anything wrong.

But she was guilty, and so was I because I got roped into her world. Being an only child with a single mother tends to do that to a young boy. I could've said no, refused to do it, and just taken my beating, but I didn't and for that I'm just as guilty as her.

She was too drunk to drive. I was too young to drive. There was no upside to this particular morning. I stopped her from leaving the house. She was still in her robe and slippers, keys gripped tightly in her hand. I grabbed the keys, figured this was where I'd draw the line. She gave me a look I'd never seen before. It was equal parts desperation and rage.

"You got two choices. Drive me to the store or give me them damn keys and get the hell outta my way!"

I, we, stood outside looking at each other. I knew I couldn't win this duel. This showdown wasn't going to have a winner. It was just a matter of picking the least wrong option.

Her license had been suspended last year when she got stopped while driving drunk. Good thing I wasn't in the car or else she would've gotten locked up and then I'd be on my own. I wasn't going to let that happen; I refused to be shipped off to some distant relative just because she couldn't steady a steering wheel.

I got in the car and turned the ignition slowly, like if I tried hard enough not to make much noise, no one would notice that a fifth grader was behind the wheel. It was a blue Cadillac, a real piece of shit. The trunk could fit about ten people in it and the brakes squealed every time they were used. The back bumper was full of dents and various colors from other cars. She always got into accidents; usually after leveling off.

The back roads could only take us so far. Eventually I had to get on the main strip to get downtown. The quickest place was a liquor store in the bad part of town. By the time I was seven I knew all of the liquor stores within a twenty-mile radius. Mom had given me the grand tour.

The road quickly became full with cars. My grip on the wheel tightened and sweat dropped from my brow. I tapped on the gas pedal every so often to jerk the car forward in random increments and rode the brakes when-ever we were going downhill. I kept one eye on the road and the other rotated between her beside me and the rearview mirror.

I heard the car before I saw it. The sirens scared me. I jumped from my seat a bit, like I was watching a scary movie in a theater. I looked over at Mom. She didn't move a muscle. She just sat there looking straight ahead at something I couldn't see. As the cop approached, she whispered for me to stay quiet and look straight ahead, that she'd take care of everything. For a minute I thought she'd figure it out, hoped that she would protect us.

The cop didn't even ask for license or registration when I rolled the window down. One look into my eyes and he told me to step out of the car. As I did, Mom yelled.

"Told you not to fucking look at him. Dumbass!"

The cop led me to the back bumper and told me to sit there and wait. He went to the passenger side. He tried to open the door but it was locked. This was her way of making things better. It was like watching an adult trying to discipline an unruly child. He knocked on the window and told her to unlock the door or else he'd break it. She did and he yanked her out of the car and pushed her back towards me.

"Alright, alright, I'm going. Get your hands off of me!"

"Shut up lady. You wanna tell me just why it is that you got a boy driving you around?"

Nothing, no answer, not even a peep out of her. She was looking at the ground.

"Lady, I asked you a question."

"You know, I've got a name."

"Yeah, well, we'll get to that in a minute. Now answer my question."

"I just wasn't feeling good and my son here was driving me to get my medicine. I'm sorry sir, it won't happen again."

"Medicine? What kind of medicine? You just passed a hospital and two pharmacies not a mile ago."

The cop brushed past us and went to the front of the car. He ducked his head inside and came out with a few small empty bottles. It was over. He'd gotten a hard look on his face, one of those tough guy looks from the movies that always meant nothing good was about to happen.

The rest of that day went by in a series of flashes that didn't seem real. At least it felt like I was looking in on someone else's troubles. I couldn't do anything; I had no power and Mom's power had been taken away from her when they had to call a second car out to the scene just to subdue her. It took two men to cuff her and a third cop just to drag her into the backseat. Drivers slowed their cars down as they passed by to watch, to put themselves into our lives for a moment as voyeurs. I kept my head down, hoping that none of my classmates were passing by.

I went with the cop in the front seat. Mom was still yelling in the backseat. It sounded more like barking actually. She yelped and spit and kicked all the way to the police station. And she screamed and punched and fell to the floor on the way to the county jail. Once she was processed, I was driven back to the police station.

"Where's your father?"

"I don't know."

"Well, where does he work?"

"I haven't seen him in four years."

"Well, who can we call that will look after you?"

I thought about it. I didn't have many options and none of them were appealing. I asked if I could spend the night at the police station and then go home the next day and get all the phone numbers and do it then. The cop looked at me, his face now back to normal, even a bit sensitive, and said that'd be fine as long as I promised never to pull a stunt like I did with the car ever again. I shook his hand

and he went and grabbed me chips and a soda from the vending machine. I slept in a holding cell that night. I had a blanket and the place was nice and warm. The bench was unforgiving but at least I knew my mom wouldn't be waking me up, desperate for some booze.

The next morning, the cop drove me back to my house. He came inside with me as I got Mom's address book out of her wallet. On the ride back to the station I asked him about my mom, if she was in big trouble.

"You should definitely call a family member. Make sure it's someone that you trust and love and wouldn't mind being with for a long time."

We stopped at a red light and he looked back at me through the rearview mirror. I couldn't hold eye contact, I was embarrassed. Embarrassed about my drunk mother, about the fact that my father could be anywhere, embarrassed that I'd been caught driving, that I couldn't even do that one simple task right.

I wanted to push out the door and run, run until the cop was out of sight, run until my feelings were out of mind, run until I couldn't move another step, run to tire myself into a deep sleep that would let me slumber through

Mom's time in jail, just run and run until they stopped looking for me and I could find a place where I wasn't known as that lady's kid.

A PROMISE IS NOTHING MORE THAN A FUTURE REGRET

The promise of a new year and a fresh start are accompanied by drunken assertions of ways to better yourself. The lingering regrets from a year gone by wasted are deafening, swollen by procrastination and laziness. Stray pine needles adorn the scuffed-up hardwood floor. Patterned wrapping paper thrown about, showcasing the impatience of a holiday gathering.

Over the course of a week's time you found out if you were naughty or nice and kissed a stranger under the mistletoe. Such a clusterfuck of imagined holidays always throws off your equilibrium. This time of year makes you feel like you're trapped in a perpetual loop of some Disney movie, where despite the false starts and obstacles, you're hoping for a happy ending. But deep in the background, if you look close enough, there are signs. Warnings about an unsatisfied life spent going through the motions.

As the hangover from the first day of the New Year wears off, you're left wondering what to make of your decisions. You reassess your future, attempt to contextualize your past behavior, and remind yourself to utilize the present to the best of your ability. By mid-month you'll be back with your ex. You'll be dependent on him, clinging to his every word, wondering how you could make the same mistake once again.

You'll go looking for answers in all the wrong places. It sounds like a country song but that doesn't ease the pain. You'll hole up under the covers, trying to stave off the cold gusts of an impersonal winter storm outside. You'll take those quizzes that are used as filler in those magazines, that don't mean much until you need something to hang onto. You'll even ask Yahoo and comb through pages of a Google search as you wonder why you're back with him, why you're so content on settling, and what that says about you.

The lack of answers scares you at first, but as the winter storms mesh into one large, continuous attack, you realize that you're being your winter self. Burrowing into a comfortable life, draping yourself in familiar surroundings. He's not what's important after all, it's the mere act of hiding; closing yourself off from the snow and ice, that's what's important.

You stay indoors, content to make the best of it, like an animal waiting for the break of spring. Until then, you gaze out the window and count the snowflakes as they slowly cascade towards their inevitable death on the dirty sidewalk. You and he are sort of like that, you think to yourself. You the beautiful, innocent snowflake, and he the dirty pile of brownish winter accumulation below, waiting, ready to swallow you whole.

Each day is one closer to freedom, to the ability to break out of this winter sluggishness. As the drips of the icicles outside your window splash against the ground you count, count the ways you've done wrong, count the days until January melts into April. Your spring self is anxious to shed your winter mistakes.

PART TWO

SUPERHERO

Caldwell was playing in the backyard with his best friend, Brian, on the day when he stopped believing in made-up stuff. Until then he had lived much of his childhood through the pages of Superman comics. Caldwell loved him. In fact, if it weren't for Superman having such perfectly combed hair in the comics, he would've never let his mother fuss over his hair in the mornings before school. Most of all, he envied Superman's powers. Caldwell hoped that maybe, if he memorized every Superman comic, he'd magically be able to fly one day.

Caldwell liked Brian because he was tough and had stood up to another kid who tried to bully Caldwell on the playground at school. Brian was four years older than Caldwell. Rumor was that he had even had sex. Caldwell thought it was cool that an older boy from down the street wanted to hang out with him. Brian's parents had much more money than his family, which meant that he had all the good toys. He had every issue of *Superman*, which made him the coolest kid ever by Caldwell's standards.

Caldwell's mother didn't like Brian, but she didn't say anything because she liked seeing her boy happy. Caldwell didn't have any other friends. His mother figured that anything was better than him staying inside by himself. But Caldwell still couldn't understand why she spent so much time worrying about whom he was hanging out with. He was eight and could take care of himself. Caldwell had been taking care of the family dog, Butch, since they got him. In fact, he was the only one who ever did anything for that dog and no one even had to remind him to do it. He'd gotten the dog from the shelter only a year before. He overheard the lady at the store tell his mother that no one wanted him. That's why Caldwell chose him. He was all alone at the shelter. Unpopular and invisible, just like Caldwell.

They were playing hide and seek. Brian had told Caldwell when they first met that he was cool because he was the best at playing the game. Caldwell had heard what everyone at school said about Brian—that he was strange and quiet and aggressive, and was always getting in trouble—but that didn't matter to Caldwell. Brian had always been nice to him.

It was Brian's turn to hide. He usually hid behind the huge oak tree down by the stream that was on the edge of his property line. Caldwell's mom warned him not to go down there by himself. But Caldwell decided that the woods were going to be his new hangout from that day forward because she only forbade him when it came to the really cool stuff, like watching television and staying up past his bedtime.

After twenty minutes of looking, Caldwell couldn't find Brian and was ready to give up. Gnats were beginning to bite his sweaty neck, which was turning red from scratching. He knew Brian would make fun of him if he went inside, but it was hot, and he was tired of zigzagging around the yard under the sun.

Caldwell heard a faint chuckle coming from the other side of the stream. It had to be Brian. Caldwell was cautious as he tiptoed across the water. The house on the other side of the stream belonged to a grumpy old man who had lost his mind long ago. Caldwell overheard his parents talking about how he was sent away for some time upstate. He didn't know what that meant but it couldn't have been a good thing because the only time he went upstate was to see his mother's father in a rest home. He hated those trips. Pop-Pop lost his hearing a while back, forcing Caldwell to yell, "I love you" so loud that it embarrassed him. He always smelt bad; like mothballs, stale lotion, and smoke.

Caldwell noticed some of the bushes moving back and forth as he reached the old man's yard. He never took good care of his yard: there were overgrown bushes as big as Caldwell, and the grass was knee-high. Caldwell had to hold in his laughter as the thick brush tickled his shins.

His amusement turned to shock as he made out Brian's figure in the distance. He was standing over a limp pile of what looked to be an animal. It was too big to be a cat but it looked too weird to be a dog; somehow more rugged and untamed. He immediately recognized the color of the fur but didn't register that it could be true. Even the screams coming from the body sounded familiar. Loud barks slowly turned into muffled moans.

Caldwell locked eyes with Brian. He had a mischievous grin on his face. A long, thick tree branch was dangling from Brian's bruised right hand. A dark red pattern was splattered across the front of his white T-shirt.

A slight whimpering noise was coming from Brian's feet. As Caldwell came closer, he noticed that the animal's thick coat of white fur was stained with the same dark red that was all over Brian. The animal's breathing was becoming more inconsistent. Heavy grasps for air were followed by sudden bursts of deep panting. Caldwell had no words to mute out the disturbing sounds.

A part of Caldwell was hoping that somehow this was all a big, cruel joke directed at him. Maybe Brian had staged this whole thing just to see what he would do. Caldwell shook these thoughts out of his head as he focused on the pile of fur at Brian's feet. This much he couldn't have staged. He'd stopped walking. He didn't want to get too close. Caldwell couldn't help wondering if this type of thing always happened back here. Maybe his mother knew that all along and wanted to shelter him from the woods.

He didn't have the time to think anymore. Caldwell knew he needed to do something. He thought of Superman, who always stood up and took a stand when something bad was happening. He wouldn't let this type of thing happen. Sure, it might be a close call, but always, at the last second, he'd swoop in and save the day. This was Caldwell's chance to do the same. He had to stand up to Brian. But Caldwell's mind and body were separate entities now. The more his mind raced, the more paralyzed he became. Fear had overtaken him. There'd be no last-minute heroics.

Without a word, Brian reached back with his right arm and brought it down towards the animal in one quick motion. The branch broke in two as it thumped against the animal's ribcage. The impact was so great that it lifted the animal from the ground for a second before it hit the ground with a dull thud. The animal was motionless, limp on its side.

Brian dropped the branch to his side, wiped saliva from the side of his mouth, and began walking towards Caldwell.

Tears formed in the corners of Caldwell's eyes and his hands were trembling. He tried his best to stay calm. Muttering to himself that Superman never showed any signs of panic, Caldwell focused his efforts on watching every move Brian made.

Brian stopped for a moment as he came within arm's reach of Caldwell, simply looked him square in the eyes, and gave him a wink. He pushed past him and headed home. No comic-strip dialogue bubble. No great, intense hand-to-hand combat scene. Just second-guessing and silence. Even the birds in the trees fell silent.

Butch remained on his side. Caldwell took a deep breath and went to get a closer look. He was dead. Bugs were already crawling through his bloody fur by the time Caldwell let out his first scream of sadness. He felt helpless. For the first time in his short life, he realized that he could never be a superhero like Superman.

He snuck back inside through the basement door and went to his room, leaving Butch out in the woods. He couldn't face going to his mother right now. She would've punished him for disobeying her. He had bigger things to worry about anyway.

He took all of his secondhand comic books and Superman posters and threw them out immediately. And even though he vowed to never read another Superman comic, he still wished that he could have special powers for that one moment and use his cape to fly into the air and not stop until he was somewhere very far away, somewhere where everything wasn't as screwed up.

ONE-HIT WONDER

Johnny's storytelling career was finished before it even really began. Cut short, like an amateur out of time at an open mic night. He never saw it coming, didn't stand a chance. He wasn't even able to finish his first one.

He didn't have to be choosy about his story, considering his audience. A pile of G.I. Joes crammed into matchbox cars and some Marvel comic superheroes gave him their full attention. They were never too busy for him like his parents. Dad was usually at work and when he was home, he sat in front of the television, beer in hand, watching anything so long as it meant he didn't have to talk. Mom wasn't much better. She stayed at home all day and watched soap operas or talked on the phone with her other homebound friends. During commercials she'd tidy up the house or put a load of laundry in the washing machine, just enough to keep up appearances.

Even though Johnny was only seven, people told him he was very mature for his age. Neighbors, family friends, teachers would all remark on his intelligence and the fact that he was so well-behaved. A few years ago, the conversation was centered on how big he was getting, as if it were such a surprise, like he shouldn't be growing. Before that it was all about how cute he was and before that he couldn't remember.

It began with a song, that much he knew. His mom loved to listen to music, she'd sing along to pass the time during Dad's absences. The record player was off-limits. It didn't matter how mature or well behaved he was. It wasn't fair that he didn't get to play with the record player, considering she'd turn it all the way up. It was like she was flaunting her possession, refusing to share. Women's voices, with deep bass and a smooth horn, would echo throughout the rooms. Scratchy crackling sounds broke up the subtle beauty of the music. So did his mom's horrible, raspy voice. Her smoke-filled lungs coughing up half-hearted renditions of the soulful pleas booming out of the speakers. The sounds began to blend together after a while. But it was the stories, the words behind the sounds, that gave them their meaning. The ladies, whom his mom never met, could keep her attention all afternoon with their stories. He wanted that type of power, that self-generated control.

Johnny never had a special talent. No particular knack or aptitude for anything specific. He wasn't dumb, but he wasn't gifted. Growing up talentless and mediocre was worse than being the slow kid in class. At least then he'd never know what he was missing out on. He was a lonely boy. He didn't have any sports teams to bond with his peers over. He had no clubs or instruments that he played and could share with a neighbor. It was just himself and his imagination.

The narrative was short, small in scope. He was timid and unsure of himself, of his voice and his own mind's capacity. It was about a balloon, mustard yellow in color and huge. Half his size but with a long thread allowing it to stream high into the clouds without getting lost. Johnny never had a balloon, not even for a birthday. That's how it started. At first the story was just about something he wanted. After a few sentences, he could hear his own voice tremble with insecurity over where the story was going.

Secretly wondering if his action figures had already lost interest, he inserted a character, a person guiding the balloon. The character was like himself, similar age, but unnamed because that didn't really matter. What mattered was that he had this big balloon that was the envy of all of his classmates. Even the adults in the town were jealous of the boy. Rumor was that he'd had the balloon for over a year without it losing any of its size. Not an inch in circumference or an ounce of helium slipped through the bottom of it. The boy came to be proud of its ability to survive. He took it to school with him, either leading it or letting it lead him, depending on the wind that particular day.

Johnny took a deep breath, searching for the next twist in the story. He didn't realize it, but as he spoke up again he turned the story into one destined for a sad ending. One day the boy woke up and went out to the mailbox, balloon in hand. As he reached his hand into the mailbox, he let go of the balloon. Before he realized what had happened, it was out of his reach, floating high above him, destined for the clouds.

Johnny stopped mid-thought, momentarily forgetting about his audience. Why had he made the story turn out the way it did? Maybe the boy was being punished for having to be an adult. Being forced to retrieve the mail instead of being allowed to play. He tossed around his action figures, erasing all clues to his secret show, and got ready for dinner.

Dinner that night was quiet. His dad emitted the usual grunts in lieu of responses to his mom's questions about his day. She gave up after a few questions, like she usually did. Johnny's thoughts remained on the lost balloon. He couldn't escape it, no matter how much applesauce he poured over his pork chop. It just didn't seem fair that no one ended up with the yellow balloon. He finished his food quickly and went to his room. He slept the yellow balloon away with thoughts of ice cream and cartoons.

When he woke up the next morning, Johnny was still trying to piece together an ending to the story. He wanted a destination for the balloon and a satisfying conclusion for the boy. He glanced over the puzzles and clues on the back of the cereal box and slurped the rest of the multi-colored milk left from the bowl. It made the sound that his mom hated. She said it was disgusting and rude.

Deep breaths, no pressure, you can do this, he said as he locked his door. He looked around the room at his figurines. He lined each one up meticulously, shoulders touching ever so slightly. Nothing was coming to him. Out of desperation he went to the window to search for something beyond the four walls of his room. His house was second from the corner. A truck passed by on the main road just a few yards up the street, and behind it emerged something strange. A giant yellow balloon appeared from nowhere in particular. The wind created from the truck's speed caused the balloon to hop up into the air, as if taking off in flight. It must've been on a neighbor's lawn or something, just rolling around, because now it was already even with the neighbor's roof and climbing steadily.

At first he didn't believe what he was seeing. He had a momentary urge to jump out the window and chase after it. Like in his story, the balloon had a lengthy rope, which at this point was still dragging along the ground. Within a few seconds the rope began to take to the sky, following the balloon.

Johnny watched the balloon for as long as he could. Eventually it was out of sight, somehow managing not to get caught up in the tree branches. Soon it was nothing more than a tic-tac in the clear morning sky. Then... nothing. He lingered by the window, half curious to see if there would be a boy about his age chasing after the balloon. There was nobody in sight. It was as if he didn't exist in this replay of his story.

Johnny turned around and dropped to the floor. Back against the wall, he began hyperventilating. He caught sight of one of his G.I. Joes, unflinching and impatient for another story. The whole bunch of them were waiting. He had never felt this kind of pressure before. His crowd remained silent, unblinking, as the seconds ticking off his bedside clock became more audible.

He'd finally found something that he enjoyed doing and now this. *Just my luck*, he thought. Maybe this was a sign? Maybe he should be outside like all of the other boys his age, getting dirty, sweating off his nervous energy until it was time for dinner. But that wasn't him, never had been. The sight of that balloon continued to flash in his head. Every time he blinked, the insides of his eyelids projected that yellow balloon. Soon there was a soundtrack to go along with it. Circus music began playing in his head.

He crawled over to his toys and toppled them all over in one motion. They made a slight thump as they hit the carpet. He took them by the handful and brought them over to his closet on the other side of the room. He found his suitcase, a hideously colored thing that he'd only used once when his family flew to Florida to visit his grandparents. He began filling it up. Three trips and the case was full. He took one last look before shutting it and locking the handle. He kicked it as hard as he could but it barely moved. Another few strikes and it reached the back of the closet. He ripped the blanket off his bed and threw it over the suitcase. Out of sight, out of mind, he hoped. He'd outgrown his childhood in a matter of minutes. No more toys, no more weird hobbies to help pass the time and fill his boredom.

Johnny unlocked his door quietly. He didn't want to garner any attention. He ducked his head out and looked down both sides of the hallway. No sight of his mother. She was probably parked in front of the television, busy doing nothing again. He wanted to join her and not have to think about anything.

She was on the couch in her bathrobe. The television was on but there was no sound. A record was playing, one of her favorites. Years of use had morphed the husky, smoke-filled voice into a slightly off-tune, manly grumble. Johnny found it easy to escape, to lose himself in the sea of background music produced by a faceless band. The lyrics weren't important anymore. Johnny relished the decisiveness in her voice, her ability to command an entire room. At least someone could.

His mother remained silent and unmoved, like his presence hadn't changed anything. She fingered her soft pack of Parliament Light 100s. She found a stubbed-out, half-smoked butt in the bottom of the pack. It was bent, forcing her to light it somewhere below her chin. She inhaled, sat back, closed her eyes, and let the smoke escape slowly from her nose like a content mother bull.

Bob Barker was goading players into overbidding for superfluous items. Everything looked so contrived to Johnny, so manufactured, so unlike real life. He wondered if he'd ever have reason to smile as wide as the chubby housewife from some no-name Midwestern town who had just won a pair of water skis.

He vowed to find another hobby, something more active, something that wouldn't leave him feeling disappointed. Nothing specific was coming to him. He knew he would never be able to finish that first story.

No follow-up, no encore. He was a one-hit wonder, just like the kind of singers his mother liked. That was enough for him for now.

THEY WENT

They went because they couldn't say no to him. He was a dominant figure, one whom nobody wanted to anger. Physically bigger than the rest and much more intelligent, he was the easy choice for group leader. He wielded his power silently, only speaking up if the situation warranted it. He projected confidence, refused to let weakness or doubt encroach. His word was absolute. It had been that way since grade school. The rest of them fell in line, devouring every word, every move he made. They were anxious for a leader, something to fill their lives with importance. Something to plug the void.

They went because they had nowhere else to go. No home to speak of, no family awaited their arrival. Their collective emptiness sustained them, brought them closer together. It lifted them up. They had to create their own family, their own sense of love through brotherhood. No one was going to provide for them. They were latchkey kids, free to roam the neighborhood. All of their fathers worked at the local plant and many of their mothers worked odd jobs as waitresses or secretaries. Their houses were small and decrepit. The rooms were full of outdated appliances and secondhand knickknacks, their parents fearful of parting with anything of potential future worth. They'd been taught to repurpose things. Frugality reigned supreme. Survival was their religion. The ability to get through another day was the only trait passed down. Arguments filled the house, erupted at a moment's notice. They drowned out the television, bounced off the walls, echoed late into the night. Money and bad luck were the topics of choice, playing routinely in front of them like a taped soap opera. To their parents they were burdens, more mouths to feed.

They went because they were bored. They sought adventure, attempted to create excitement out of nothing. Their neighborhood weighed down all of the inhabitants, slowly eroded their confidence. It eventually got the better of them too. Youthful exuberance was no match for generations of disappointment. It was in the air, it quietly hovered over all of them. You could see it in their eyes. Dreams were delayed in favor of an unspoken sense of gratitude for what little they had. No one told them that they could have something, anything more. An attitude of being inferior lingered. They perpetuated the myth with each silent day that passed. They spent the day drunk from forties of stolen malt liquor and full of nicotine from their fathers' cigarettes. Boredom was filled with fights amongst themselves. The outcomes were predetermined; a hierarchy had already been set within their own group. Clenched fists were their secret handshake. They longed for the taste of blood on their lips and looked forward to the formation of bruises on their faces. It awoke them, brought them together, and kept the outside world at a distance.

They went because they were curious. Their hangouts were limited to the bodega, the basketball court, and the quarry. It was the nicest thing that came out of the town. A historical oasis among the modern ruins. People spoke about it in hushed tones. Teachers warned students about it. The cops routinely patrolled it, as a way to justify their salaries. It was a rite of passage for all of the young boys since the First World War. It represented an escape from the cracked sidewalks, boarded-up houses on Main Street, and empty parking lots. It was illegal to enter: there were threats of arrest for trespassing because it was owned by the local power plant. That just further fueled the desire, the need to explore. Fenced off and surrounded by large, overgrown brush and trees, the site had multiple entryways. If examined thoroughly by someone determined not to be refused admittance, it was easy enough. They had built a vision of it in their heads over the years. Each time the structure loomed larger, became more monumental. They were anxious to see if it lived up to years of expectation fueled by the legends recounted by their older brothers and cousins.

They went, finally. It was the start of summer, the first really hot day of the year. They were dressed in cut-off jean shorts because they couldn't afford their own swimwear. Hand-me-downs from older siblings or raided from their fathers' wardrobes. They scraped together enough money for pot and beer. This was a celebration, their white trash Bar Mitzvah. Everyone wanted to replicate the adventures overheard from their brothers. To somehow outdo what the older ones had previously done. They followed their leader; the group walked in silence. The only sounds audible were their worn shoes as they hit the pavement. The gravel changed to dirt as they followed the worn path to the fence. The cut in the fence was big enough for just one at a time.

They went to the edge of the cliffs. The dirt morphed to pure white sand beneath them. The density of the brush and trees slowly evaporated as they neared. It was really as high as they had been told, maybe higher. As they reached the edge of the first cliff, they stood in wonder at the sight below them. The coral blue water was unlike anything they had ever seen before. Never had they imagined that their neighborhood could produce something so gorgeous. They could see straight through to the bottom. It looked shallow, too shallow to jump in. They were buoyed by thoughts of previous generations that had taken the plunge before them. The first overhang was sixty feet high. They only needed a few drinks to produce the courage to leap.

The leader went first. He casually dropped off the lip. He emerged from the water with a smirk. Beads of water ran down his face. The others fought to follow him in, down into the water below, away from their troubles on the mainland.

They went despite the unknown. They skipped the second cliff at the leader's request. The highest one was well over one hundred feet tall. Confidence oozed from his pores. He was drunk with poise, eager to impress his brothers. It was much steeper than he expected. This time he jumped forward, leapt off the edge with a giant push that began at the bend in his knees. Then time. Stood. Still.

He stayed in the air for ten seconds. The group shuffled to the edge, excited to witness, to be a part of.

He hit the water on his side, ribs exposed. The water smashed against his body, reluctant to accept his arrival. The others remained quiet, looked on, waited for him to re-emerge. Any moment now. He never did. Minutes passed. The group was frozen, paralyzed without their leader. The next oldest ran down to the first cliff and plunged in headfirst.

They went home changed forever. The youngest one panicked and called the cops. No one had time to clean up their mess. Full on beer and pot, empty of emotions, they sat and waited, listened, as the sirens grew louder. The police led them back onto the street, hands gripped tightly around their wrists to make sure they wouldn't try and run. Firemen, paramedics, and a search and rescue diving team ran by, plowed through the fence, moved quickly through the brush. It all happened so fast. A crowd of people formed across the street in the parking lot of the church. They found him later that afternoon. It took three divers to pull him up from the bottom. He broke his neck, shattered his ribcage, and punctured a lung on impact. He died instantly.

They went home in cop cars. Silent and leaderless, the boys tried to hold back their tears. Their fathers were ready for them at home, belts in hand. They waited for the cops to leave and the door to close.

The rest of the summer went by in a quiet haze. They healed their bruises and remembered their fallen leader. Nothing would ever be the same again. It was the end of their group. They were alone, on their own. None of them stepped up and became the leader of the group. By the start of the school year they had all gone their own way. There was nothing to hold them together. Memories of their fallen leader were conjured up every time they saw one another. It was too hard.

They went many places after that, alone, but they never did go back to the quarry again.

UNLACED AND FITTED

I found out about his death while on Facebook. I was idly checking out photos of cute girls who were friends of friends. The news stunned me, brought me back to the moment. I realized that I hadn't seen him in years, almost a decade. Way back when we carried our CDs around and logged into MySpace and AOL chat rooms.

A page memorializing him was set up. Mostly just one-line sympathies and thoughts, idle prayers sent to the parents who probably would never access the page. I recognized many of the names, mostly high school friends that I had lost touch with the summer after school. I began clicking on pictures of people who posted, once friends and now just sort of cyber-acquaintances. I quickly veered far away from the page and deeper into the maze of my former classmates' inner lives. What grad schools they were attending, where they went for summer vacation, what internships they had landed. It was all just enough to keep me distracted from the fact that my best friend from high school, Christian, had died.

I found it odd that, from this news, I was just one click away from pivoting to links of music videos and photos of a Friday night spent out in the city getting drunk. The proximity of everything in my news feed startled me. It hadn't occurred to me before this. This was my first experience with death in the Internet age. The emotions seemed less real through the lens of social media. In a way I felt as if Christian's life, his memory, was competing for space and time and it was a battle he was bound to lose. The hyper-cycle of information, the ever-changing nature of Facebook in general, was at direct odds with the attempt to capture and freeze his life, this moment of loss. This fragmented bombshell was quickly lost amidst the links and videos and updates.

His younger sister, Julia, had set up the page. Her presence seemed muted, even inconspicuous. The page had little info other than a link to the online news article about his death and his obituary a few days after. She posted photos of her brother. Checking the timeline, it was clear that she had posted everything almost in succession. One big dump of the photographic remnants of his life, a few dozen in total, a clear sign that she emotionally threw up on the page immediately after his death and then left the page for others. Most were of him alone, reiterating his solitary personality. A few baby pictures were thrown in with the batch—a black and white photo of him with his family, as a young boy, was clearly photocopied from a family photo album. I began to wonder what she was feeling when she went to the local stationery store to copy the photo, how she processed not only the sudden loss but her duty to memorialize him somehow in her own small way.

Julia was only a few years younger than us. We shared the same school for my final two years of high school. I'm not sure if it was the age difference or the fact that she was my best friend's sister, but I never really tried to get to know her. She was quiet and always had a book in her hand or homework in front of her. Despite spending more time with Christian than anyone, I didn't know much about her, his only sibling. We rarely made it past the obligatory greetings, and when we did, the conversation was dominated by silence, those awkward moments where I was searching for the right phrase to put her at ease and she was itching to just get away, to be anywhere but right there, right then. I never pushed it. She was a lot like her brother in that respect. If you couldn't break through the wall of defense at first, then you stood little chance of ever getting to know her.

Even though they lived in a small house, Christian and Julia had separate bedrooms. Christian had to change what originally was the living room closet into his own make-shift bedroom. He hung a sheet in lieu of a door for some semblance of privacy. When that didn't work, he found some scrap wood and put together a door to distance his adolescence from the rest of the house. It was crooked and wobbly, the wood flimsy and uneven. The bottom of his door was about six inches from the ground. It looked like a really bad imitation saloon door, but it was his and he was proud of cornering off his own space in the cramped house. It was big enough for a twin mattress and a few empty crates to hold his computer and records. He slept on top of his wardrobe.

Christian died in a car crash. A drunk driver veered into his lane and hit him head on. He must've died on impact because the paper didn't mention anything about a hospital.

It was early in the morning. He was on his way to work. He was one of the few from our class who had remained in town, working for the village parks and recreation department.

The driver survived, unjustly, cruelly. He was being treated at the hospital. I pictured expensive tests being run, all paid for by his insurance. Expert doctors and pleasant nurses working round the clock to keep alive this taker of a human life. It didn't seem fair, none of it did.

I would've gone to the hospital myself and pulled the plug, smothered him with a pillow, any of the clichés, but I couldn't. The paper mentioned, briefly, that after he stabilized, he would be transferred to the county jail and held on bail. They said cops were stationed outside of his room, securing it for his safety as well as to ensure the proper transfer from medical to correctional facilities. He was in a cocoon, bubbled off from the damage he'd created. He was no longer a man; he was a number. He'd go from a bracelet ID to a number on the back of his orange jumpsuit. That wasn't good enough for me, for Christian's memory, for our friends, but it was all we had.

The final paragraph was vague on details. Just a few short sentences about Christian, whom he left behind, a favorite hobby listed (basketball); another favorite hobby (smoking weed and getting drunk) was omitted. The piece mentioned that plans were in motion for Christian's funeral. The driver would undoubtedly get dozens of bylines. Court cases, appeals, bail hearings, sentencing. The remnants of his actions would fill our local paper, taunting Christian's family in black and white long after Christian's memory had faded from the town's conscience. Beat reporters would be assigned to the man as if he were an event, the exercise voyeuristic at its core: a form of grief porn.

I shut the paper in a fit of rage. I needed to re-contextualize the scenario. Paint it in a different light. The truth was too glum to sit with.

The irony of the whole thing hit me square in the gut, somewhere below my ribcage. The facts of that morning rattled around, echoing with increasing reverberations as the blank spots began to fill in. I thought back to how we spent the majority of high school. Drunk and in motion. A whirl of spinning images backed by a vodka taste on our tongues. He would drive despite double vision, claiming to be better at navigating the twisting two-lane roads of our neighborhood. "It's simple, just close one eye and steer towards the middle," he would say when the car would go momentarily silent as the CD player switched songs. We never did get in a crash. Together we seemed safe, skirting the law and the odds. The protection of ignorant teenage bliss, strength in numbers, whatever it was, it was with us. Was this some form of payback? I didn't have the nerves or the patience to try and unravel that question.

A quick search found plenty of information on the driver. The accidental killer. His name was Josh Wilson, a name so generic that it only perpetuated the fantasy element of the whole incident. Maybe it wasn't real after all, just one big nightmare. But as I delved deeper, hoping to find something, anything to justify my rage towards this man whom I'd never met, I began to experience something completely unexpected: empathy.

I couldn't tell if I had found the right person based on his generic profile picture. It was a sports logo of his favorite football team. At first I thought I had found the wrong Wilson, a teenage version. Scrolling down, though, confirmed that this was the right person. His wall was littered with angry postings and outright threats. A few of the names were familiar, former schoolmates and mutual friends. Most of the anger came with a profile picture, a link back to the source of the rage. The threats, however, were mostly from faceless thumbnails, accounts set up for the sole purpose of electronically venting frustration. Faceless bullying and intimidation that I thought stopped after leaving high school.

His profile page was set to public, allowing me unfettered access to this portion of his life. He had more friends than I did, almost two thousand in fact. There were countless albums of backyard barbeques (beer in hand smiling with his buddies), Little League games, and family vacations. He had three young kids and a pretty wife. Their lives now shattered as well.

Pete sent me an email shortly after Christian's death. It was simple and straight to the point, much like Pete himself. He said that he needed to meet up with me, preferably before Christian's funeral, to talk. Pete was a townie, like Christian and me. The details, at that moment, weren't important to me. It was just good to see a familiar face, one free from the pathetic and insular privileged lives of the majority of our classmates.

We met at the local bar on Main Street, across from the firehouse. We were the only people in the place without gray hair. The jukebox, the pool table; it was all too simple and familiar. I hadn't been there in years. It was the first place to serve us back in high school. We were only sophomores. That didn't matter. I still remember the bartender that night leaning in and mumbling *Just don't start acting stupid*, then winking before sliding over a few bottles of beer and a couple shots of whiskey.

Although I'd run into Pete in town every so often since high school, something about our friendship had changed. I suppose it had a lot to do with me, with the broken promises, the stealing, the drugs, and the disappointment. Nothing bonded us together anymore. No longer teammates, no more shared sacrifice or common goals. We drifted even before school ended. As our classmates moved on to exclusive liberal arts schools, our friendship, that chapter of it at least, ended altogether. We both knew that everything had changed and yet we were both here, stuck in town, idling like a beat-up Cadillac.

We'd both gained considerable weight, he from a steady stream of cold beer and I from cutting out my daily high school diet of cocaine and heroin. He still showed signs of his former self, reminders of a once athletic body with his thick, broad shoulders and powerful legs. He already had some drinks lined up on the counter when I walked in.

"What up man?"

"Same shit, you know. Just trying to get by."

Already, in my mid-twenties, this town had reduced me to the vernacular of a middle-aged man, full of regrets and one-liners to try and explain away the dreary reality of my situation.

"I got you a drink. Still a beer and whiskey guy, right?"

"Sure."

I didn't have the heart to tell him that I'd been sober. He knew that I was clean but, not being an addict himself, didn't understand the causal link between one drink and the probability that if I took that drink, by the end of the night I'd end up down in the city waiting on the block for my dealer, needle in my arm, crack rocks in my pocket to keep me from nodding out later in the bathroom of the train coming back home.

"Tough shit about Christian man. Dude was good people."

Pete was looking straight ahead, staring at the row of liquor bottles above the bar. I pushed my drinks away from me but kept them at arm's reach.

"Yeah, took me by surprise. I feel awful for his family, especially his sister," I said.

I waited for him to work through the small talk on his own time and get to the point of why we were here.

"So, how you been? Staying out of trouble?"

"Yeah, straight and narrow. A little bit of school, you know, trying to do things right this time."

"Good to hear man, good to hear. So, how'd you find out about Christian?"

"Facebook…weird man. Still doesn't feel real," I said.

"That's why I wanted to meet up. I was actually first on the scene to the crash."

The sentence hung in the air between us, its presence taking on a life of its own. I needed to say something, anything to erase the words that hung there, stronger than the shot glass of whiskey just a reach away.

"Damn, really?"

I forgot that he was working as a paramedic for the town. For a moment my focus shifted from Christian back to myself. I was wondering how Pete, someone who was about half as smart as me, could be holding down a job and living in his own place when I was still stuck at home, unemployed.

"Yeah, it was something. Man, easily the worst I've ever seen in person. Not just because it was Christian. It looked like a scene from a movie. Metal bent like twisty straws, smoke everywhere. The worst was I didn't even know it was Christian until I found his wallet, twenty yards from the car. He was fucked up, the whole thing was. Already dead man, just lying there like a disassembled action figure, parts of him lying everywhere."

I cut him off, my stomach tumbling like a dryer.

"What's the point of this?"

"What?"

"I mean what is this? I don't want to hear this. This is fucked up, it's morose," I said.

"It's what? Well, I'm just saying, I need to get this out man. I figured you could handle it, you know, given what you've been through…Anyway, you guys were close, no one knew him like you did. I thought you'd want, no, need to hear this. I mean, no one else from school cares enough to do anything more than just post something on Facebook, you know?"

I sat there, staring into Pete's eyes. He was right, in his weird, twisted way. I'd abandoned Christian in the years since high school, much like Pete. This wasn't closure, more like proper context, some details to cling to no matter how sick. It was needed to fill in the gap of the past few years.

It took Pete's honesty to make me realize that I did want to hear everything. I wanted to know what was on the radio when Pete arrived, to see how Christian still preferred old school hip-hop to the newer stuff. I wanted to hear if he was still wearing his trademark blue jeans and white T-shirt, not giving a shit what other people thought. If he had his Timberlands on, unlaced as always. If he still had that hat, that Yankees fitted, that he wore every day to the point where it was more of a grey than a dark navy blue.

I wanted everything that I could no longer have. I wanted a second chance at staying close to Christian after we left high school. A quick look into Pete's eyes and I knew that he couldn't give me what I needed. What I needed was to go back in time and just press repeat so that our time together would never end, like those CDs that

we listened to over and over late into the night when the
world was ours.

FIREFLIES, FRESH CUT GRASS, AND THE NIGHT AIR

A cheap bottle of wine for the hosts, a carton of cigarettes for me, and a Scrabble board in case the party gets boring.

I peer in through the window on the right side of the door, looking for a familiar face inside. Take a deep breath and ring the doorbell because I'm too timid to knock.

I'm scared to ring it again. I don't want to be a bother so I go around the house, on the east end, to the backyard. I'm hoping there's someone outside.

I keep my head down, focusing on the gate latch, and let myself in. I move past my embarrassment and awkwardness and enter the backyard, hoping to slip into the crowd.

I regret bringing the bottle of wine to this group of less than welcoming people.

"Hey man, I'm good! The kids are great, getting bigger by the day. How is everything?" I rack my mind for his name but come up with nothing. The fact that he's drinking beer somehow reminds me of being at a frat party. His being more handsome and better dressed doesn't bother me as much now.

Better off I didn't know his name. I move right to the table by the fence. I take out my bottle of wine and place it amongst the other liquor. Intimidated by the high school-like cliques, I remain at the table and pour myself a drink from the bottle of wine. I decide to stand there, with my back against the fence, so I can observe the party and figure out my next move.

"Donald, actually," I say. I remain calm on the outside as my brain goes into overdrive. Who is she? What does she want? I don't really care to know the answer. I'm just happy that I'm no longer standing by myself. Starting to realize why my wife didn't want to go in the first place. I curse at myself, under my breath, wishing I could trade places with her right now and be at home in my sweats, watching movies with my kids.

"Actually, she was just diagnosed with cancer. Breast, not ovarian. She's a trooper though and she's got a great doctor so we'll see what happens." I scan the backyard, hoping to find a familiar face, anyone willing to just be. No need for small talk, just stand around and get drunk like when we were younger. I take a step back, away from her, and bump into the table. My eyes are now focused on the tops of my shoes, my forehead is starting to perspire, and my stomach is feeling queasy.

Thank God that's over, I say to myself. I kind of hoped that all of the drinks would've been spilt over, just to see everyone's reaction, to make them react to me. I have to calm down; I repeat it softly like a mantra. The faces in the yard are intimidating in their sheer numbers alone. I am one against many. I decide that I'll need another glass of wine before I move from my chosen spot.

I regret bringing the game with me. I feel childish and nerdy. What adult would sit down and actually play with me? What was I thinking? Another glass is poured by me. More fuel to quiet the internal dialogue.

The touch feels nice, less expected of me than a conversation. I wouldn't mind brushing up against more people here. Just quiet touches, I think to myself as my knees become weak. The fact that I'm a relative unknown here doesn't seem as important now.

I feel jealous of these names. Some of them are so exotic, so interesting to hear come off the lips of others. I wish my name was something cool, something that could still excite me to hear after all these years.

A bland reproduction of a name that's been handed down to offspring for centuries. Donald, like the duck; Don, like a creepy uncle.

I'm too drunk to play anything. It would've been a nice thing to do when I first arrived, to break the ice, but it's too late. Her gift has been almost emptied all by myself. Guilt overcomes me. "Hey, there you are! Actually, I did bring Scrabble with me but I'm not really in the mood. How are things?" I look to my glass, which is empty, and want to play a game where people continuously rush to fill up my glass.

"Hmmm...it's not going to be natural if you asked me to do it now, is it?" I sound like a jerk. As soon as the words leave my mouth, I cringe. I no longer care what the people here think of me.

"Good question, I'm sorry, I didn't mean to be abrasive. I'm just, well, I'm drunk." I stumble away, back towards the table, safe from everyone's expectations.

The bottle has been emptied. Just a few stray cans of domestic beer and a warm bottle of whiskey. I pick up my bag, which I stashed under the table, and grip it tightly. I want to go home where there are no social rules. No right, no wrong, just the here and now. This is why I promise myself not to drink, I tend to clam up, retreat like a defeated soldier, a wounded baby.

I search my pockets for my car keys but can't find them. They're not in my bag either. I decide to slip out the back gate as quietly as possible, resigned to coming back the next morning to find my keys.

The party, this whole night, everything that's just happened reminds me of high school. When I wasn't the popular kid, when I had to overcompensate just to feel something, to get noticed, be appreciated even if for just a moment. As the cars zoom by, I'm reminded that just because I've gotten older doesn't mean I've matured.

I have to remember that my home is not horrible, my kids are not horrible. There is a reason why I'm walking with traffic, on the side of the street in the calming darkness of night with nothing but the moon and passing headlights to guide me.

My house keys are on the same chain that my car keys were. Somewhere back in that backyard. I knock on the door. And wait for someone to wake. To let me in.

ACCIDENTAL MEMORIES

I found her by mistake. Complete accident. I'd been here a thousand times. Relegated the whole act to nothing more than a daily chore. A means to an end. This was different. This slowed me down, brought feelings to the surface. I wasn't looking for this, but I found it. I wanted to turn it off, go back to the previous page, and somehow erase her face. Click on those countless other thumbnails to diminish her presence. But I couldn't. My eyes froze, locked in place with warm memories of our common history. A familiar story, a link back to the real world.

The last time I saw her, she was signing my high school yearbook. She was crying silently, knowing that things would never be the same between us. I was going to the local state college, the only school that accepted me. She was leaving early to participate in a summer session out west at some prestigious liberal arts school. We both hoped it could continue. That we could make it work, find a way to stay connected, to continue our last year of high school indefinitely.

And it did, for a while. I had to sign up for a more expensive unlimited cell phone plan. Thoughts of infinite minutes and endless texting kept my spirits high for the moment. By the end of August, the phone calls turned to chats with her voicemail. With her busy class schedule, I was resigned to emails. Facebook chats were conducted in the early morning hours because of the time difference, further accommodating her new life. By mid-September I was logged into Facebook on my cell phone continuously, staring at the screen during freshman composition classes, anxiously waiting for her to log in. I hid the real reasons behind my postings with stories of my school and life. Slowly, the reasons for contacting her didn't matter. I began littering her wall with pleas for contact, desperate for something, anything.

The homepage advertised free fantasies. They never said anything about feelings. It was an aggregator site, free of charge. You could stream the clips to your desktop and watch, but downloading wasn't an option. They gave you momentary pleasure but took away any opportunity for sustained happiness. The inability to own the images—to turn off the computer with the knowledge that the videos would be there, waiting for me when I came back—left me always wanting more.

I was a voyeur, projecting myself into these dream scenarios. They were fleeting but powerful. She was another body in a sea of flesh. One of dozens of individual screen shots previewing hardcore action. She was wearing a lace miniskirt, knee-high stockings, and a pulled-down tank top that barely contained her breasts. Pigtails finished off her image. I was surprised they didn't have her sucking on a lollipop.

I questioned all our mutual friends while they were home for Thanksgiving. My investigation gave me a purpose, as if it could provide a chance at real answers, or at least some kind of an explanation. Word was that she dropped out of school halfway through her first semester. A friend of a friend had a cousin who went to school with her. She said that she started dating a local guy who was dealing drugs. She'd gotten into meth. She stopped hanging out with her friends before she dropped out altogether and moved in with him just off-campus.

It was a simple business model. Litter the screen with pop-up windows of ads and large banners. On the bottom corner of her video a website was highlighted in bold neon letters. I went to the site, leaving the land of free porn in my past. She was the featured girl, "newcumer of the week." I was only able to get a thirty-second trailer. If I wanted the entire forty minutes of her, I'd have to pay. As I thumbed my credit card, already maxed out from beer runs with my buddies on the weekends, I wondered if I really wanted to see what was behind the payment form. No matter how curious, I was ill equipped for it. To see her as an object, a commodity, a piece of flesh whose sole purpose was extracting pleasure from others, was soul-crushing.

I convinced myself that I would go out there and find her. Someone had to step up, do something. In my mind I relished being the good guy, playing the savior role. I imagined how the scene would unfold in my head dozens of times. I would solve everything, would right her wrongs, show her where she'd strayed. I calculated flight costs and rental cars, the weight of the numbers momentarily numbing me to the reality of the situation.

It cost me thirty dollars to see her—the girl that I planned on losing my virginity to—having sex with a stranger. She did a short interview with the cameraman before she undressed. Hearing her say our hometown out loud made me squirm. It was the first time I'd heard my nothing of a town spoken by someone else outside of Main Street. The room looked like a cheap motel and the drapes were barely open, letting in a slight landscape of brown mountains and a dusty ground. My best guess was Las Vegas or southern California.

I visited her parents first, figured it was the right thing to do. I wasn't sure how much they knew, if at all. They knew enough, too much, more than I did in fact. They'd banned her from coming home. She was on her own, totally dependent on her new boyfriend. Her father said that their family counselor thought it was for the best. Her mother stayed quiet, deferring to him, busying herself with tidying up the coffee table as I sat down in the living room. The pile of unopened mail was beginning to collect dust.

They said that she'd recently called, asking for money. They refused, apparently reciting from the agreed-upon script determined by the counselor. They looked relieved just to mention that they had heard from her. Confirmation that she hadn't died. Her father was growing firmer by the moment as his wife held back her tears. My time had expired. I was doing more harm than good bringing all this up. He walked me out to my car, the mother standing catatonic at the doorway, and warned me, "You can't help people who don't want to help themselves." I left defeated, resigned to late-night high school memories of her.

Hints of her former self shone through. Her bubbly smile, her vague answers, the way she twitched her nose when she grew nervous. Somewhere, deep down, her real self was still there. But I had to strain to find it. She looked different, a caricature of her teenage self. Her hair was full of bleached blonde extensions. Her face was sunken in on itself, as if it were trying to hide from the camera. Her chin was acne-riddled. She was rail thin; if you looked closely enough you could see the outline of her ribcage. Her breasts, once supple and modest, were inflated balloons, slightly misshapen distortions. I gagged a bit, fighting the faintest taste of warm bile back down into my gut. Her eyes were a shade of grey I didn't remember.

Countless afternoons, spent together skipping out on school to go sneak into the local movie theater or wander around the mall, came flooding back to me. We went to junior and senior prom together and were even named homecoming King and Queen. She looked like a princess in her prom dress. Everyone's eyes were on her when we were on the dance floor. The other girls were jealous of her and the guys were jealous of me for being with her. I thought after junior prom that I'd surely be able to have sex with her. She said she wanted to, but she tossed around words like "love" and "responsibility," along with conflicting terms like "not ready" and "too young." I drank myself into a stupor that night, leaving her gossiping with her girlfriends until the sun came up. I loved her, as much as I could at that age, and was willing to wait.

The eastern European Neanderthal who was sharing the screen with her oozed masculinity. His muscles bulged, stretching his upper arm tribal tattoo to its limit. His gelled hair was short and it looked as if he plucked his eyebrows. No doubt he was hung, easily twice as big as mine and much thicker. It was like a mallet, ready to inflict pain on his next assigned coed, my coed. He was a real pro, slowly tricking her into a sense of comfort before unleashing his domination.

She handled it adeptly, like she'd done it a thousand times. Stroking and caressing it into shape, becoming stern with it as it grew in her mouth. As her chin grew sloppy with spit, and his hands tightened against her scalp, roughly guiding it back and forth, her eyes deadened a bit, losing that life that I'd once fallen for. Her head bobbed violently, trying to match the guy's growing intensity. His moans descended down on her, telling her how he liked it. The dirty talk started soon after. Words like "dirty slut" and grunting affirmations of "you like that, don't you" filled the room, echoing off the smoke-stained walls.

I unzipped my pants and reached for my penis. Force of habit. The coldness of my hand scared it at first but it was too late. I began thinking of how she used to handle me. Calmly, with care, and a slight hesitation. Never going down all the way. Mostly massaging the tip, tickling the head. There were feelings involved, cheapening the lust of the moment, deadening the excitement, complicating the raw instincts that should've overtaken the situation. A token gesture meant to show her affection and somehow please me while also holding off additional advances, further violations of her pure body that we both knew I wanted.

He inserted it without hesitation. Watching him do it so quickly and without care made me squirm. I reconsidered all of my failed attempts at reaching the very same precipice. I felt trapped, suffocated within this sphere of virtual fantasy. My heart began beating faster. I could feel the blood pumping through my veins as her moans intensified. My hands were sweaty with anxiety and anticipation. My chest started to thump in unison with the background music. Her skull hit the headboard repeatedly. I was focused, squinting and inching closer to the screen for a better look. I owed her that much. I was paying her my final respects. It was the only amount of control I had left. She turned her head away from him and the camera several times. He had to grab the back of her neck to get her to look up at him. Her refusal to make eye contact was a sign, confirmation that she was, indeed, in need of money. This realization broke through the barriers of fantasy that had taken me this far. This was her job.

I zipped up my pants. I couldn't go through with it. No amount of lighting, no amount of camera manipulation, could force me to derive pleasure from her circumstances. I thought I saw tears in her eyes. That was the only emotion left. For either of us. He grabbed her by the hair, threw her to the floor in a quick whirl, like he was handling a barn animal, and finished on her face without a warning.

A forced smile, an exhausted wave, a wink to the camera, and it was all done. She looked miserable, her pigtails loosened, face glistening with sweat, mascara running down her cheeks, slowly mixing in with the congealing sperm. She looked trapped, a prisoner of male control.

The video ended abruptly. No music, no slick transition, just a black screen. The words of the website flashed in front of me, taunting me, laughing at me, a reminder of their conquest, of what I let slip away, what I lost, but most importantly, what she lost.

I downloaded the movie and saved it to my desktop. Just in case, I rationalized to myself. Tears were the only fluids that my body was capable of creating at the moment. I cried over our shared losses and missed opportunities. I found my high school yearbook. Her smile staring back up at me on the page. I studied it for minutes, every inch of her face burned into my memory, convinced that this was how she should be remembered. I deleted the movie. I clung to her smile instead, and for those few minutes, everything was fine again.

PART THREE

IDLE MUSIC

I can't listen to certain music anymore. It's just too painful. It reminds me of certain people, specific places, and times. My past is always parallel to my present and hopefully my future promises better.

Jam bands are out. She listened to them all: Phish and the Grateful Dead, Dark Star Orchestra, and My Morning Jacket. She followed them around the country like a 21st-century hippie. iPhone in hand, tie dye outfits, and unwashed hair was her uniform. She would dance barefoot until she fell from exhaustion and then search for an app to download, something, anything that would bring the sixties back.

Old school hip-hop is out. She, different one, listened to music like it was 1997. Biggie and Tupac, A Tribe Called Quest and De La Soul, Wu Tang and NWA bled from the speakers. She would drive like a maniac in a car almost as old as us. She'd pop in a tape and start rapping along with the deep voices. She made wild hand movements to no one in particular. Usually she had no hands on the wheel. She'd get pissed when it was over and the tape deck popped it out. And she'd switch coasts just like that, within hand's reach.

If they come on the radio I'll turn them off. The wounds of two past relationships in particular are too powerful, too raw. I can't shake these two girls, women, from my soul. The memories follow me like a shadow and refuse to diminish.

But every once in a while, at night when I can't sleep, I'll turn them on and jam out, rap into the mirror. I pretend that the lyrics can erase the bad memories for three minutes at a time.

OFFBEAT DRUMMER

She was in the band, well, not the band, just a band. They were opening for some slightly better known band that just got a record deal for enough money to cover their recording costs. She was the drummer.

She was wearing a dirty Black Flag sleeveless T-shirt, showing off her wiry, pale arms freckled with black and white tattoos. Her tight black jeans were barely able to contain her thick thighs. Each kick of the drum almost daring her jeans to rip at the seam. Sweat was dripping down her face, smearing what little makeup she was wearing. I wanted to jump up on stage and rub it in, draw smiley faces on her cheeks to take the edge off of her, make her a little less intimidating.

But I didn't go on stage. I didn't even approach her after their set was finished. I stayed in the corner, back to the exposed brick wall that was deemed necessary in order to charge ten dollars a beer. She ordered whiskey, took a seat at the bar, and kept her head down. She was pounding her fists against her thighs, seemingly unfulfilled from her short set. The song on the jukebox was some gutter punk song from the early nineties. Way too obscure for me. As the song's tempo amped up, her fists were joined by her feet tapping against the bar floor. Both were slightly offbeat, but that didn't seem to matter to her.

I ordered another beer, wanting to get a closer look at her. She looked more human somehow; her imperfections eased the invisible boundary that her stage presence had built. I chugged the lukewarm beer, hoping for some sort of courage, but the bottom of the bottle gave me no concrete answers, no plan of action, not even a suggestion.

It had been a while since I'd been with a girl and even longer since I tried picking one up in a bar. The song ended abruptly, leaving the chatter of conversations lingering in the air behind me. I braced myself against the open barstool, knees weak from beer and anticipation. I brushed up against her as I fell into my seat. She was still drumming, playing out the next song on the album, as the jukebox sat waiting for its next quarter.

"Sorry about that," I said.

No response, just more tapping.

I ordered another beer and a shot, for her. I handed the bartender a twenty and slid the shot glass over to her without making eye contact. I darted my hand in her direction, momentarily stopping her still twitching legs. She looked up and mumbled something but I continued to look straight ahead, staring into the rows of half-filled liquor bottles, hoping my fear wasn't as see-through as the vodka.

"Hold on a second," I said.

I took my beer, got up, and made my way to the jukebox. I played the previous song, finished my beer, and looked for her thighs. They started moving frantically again, like a puppet with a crazed master, still unable to maintain a beat. I left the bar happy just to get one last glimpse of those gorgeous thighs causing friction against the barstool.

SUBURBAN WEAPON OF MASS DESTRUCTION

It was loud, an explosion of colliding metal frames fighting to maintain their shape. Glass shattered everywhere. Tiny bits sprayed into the air, blanketing the scene like clear shards of volcanic ash. Horns triggered, beaming out an obnoxious, continuous sound as if prison security had been breached. The silent evidence of the crash was the most unsettling though. Airbags were deployed and the seatbelts were torn in half. And smoke everywhere, clouds of it pluming above us like a smoke signal warning those nearby of danger.

"Are you okay kid? Can you hear me? Does anything hurt? Don't move, I've already called for help."

The sound, coming from outside my window, began to fade away. I slipped back into sleep, my neck sore from the initial impact. Off in the distance I could hear some more talking, this time louder and more pronounced. Shrieks followed.

The actual crash didn't hurt. Not at all in fact. Nothing broken, nothing bloody except for my nose, which had more to do with the fact that I'd had a rolled-up dollar bill shoved up there for the better part of 24 straight hours. I couldn't see beyond the smoke; my vision was blurred.

When I came to, I heard the ambulance sirens. The lights had turned my sight from complete darkness to a mixture of gray and orange and red. My door was flung open violently by two men in uniforms. I thought of the show *ER* and waited for my George Clooney to appear. Instead all I got were two overweight middle-aged men.

"Can you hear us?"

I nodded, not sure if I could talk.

"What hurts? Show us where it hurts."

Nothing came specifically to mind. Just a pervasive, all-encompassing soreness throughout my body. I knew it was nothing serious. From the moment I opened my eyes after running head-on into the other car, I knew God wouldn't grant me the pleasure of dying.

I let out a faint murmur. My best attempt at a grunt.

"How much have you had to drink buddy?"

I turned my head slightly, away from the questions, and looked to my side. A pile of empty beer cans were on the passenger seat. The morning sun was shining in through the passenger window.

The rays let off a glinting sparkle when they hit the tin foil wrappers on the floor beneath the beer. I moved my hand towards the cup holder in the middle and found my needle and crack pipe.

"The cops are on their way so sit tight for a second, okay?"

I hadn't planned on going anywhere even if I could twist myself free from the metallic knot at my feet. The two men rushed back towards the other car, whose engine was now up in smoke. They helped the firemen extinguish the fire.

I was able to punch the steering wheel up a foot or so to allow me to wriggle free enough to move about the car. I reached over, as far as I could, and finally got hold of the bag of tin foil wrappers. I took them out, one by one, and began swallowing them. Eight tens of heroin and crack each, more than $150 down the hatch in two minutes. I finished the final opened beer at my side by crouching down. It was warm, tasting like fermented apple juice. I gagged just to keep everything down. All I had to do was keep it down until I got processed and bailed out. Twenty-four hours at the most. I took it as a challenge.

It kept my mind from the possible horror inside the other car.

OLIVE, DIRTIED

The neighborhood quickly changed. Rows of identical-looking, economical one-family houses gave way to expansive urban stretches of desolate lots. Everything was locked up behind imposing chains. The streetlights stopped functioning, except for a continuous yellow blinking. Sneakers were draped over telephone wire like some sort of ghetto Christmas decoration. The few houses still standing were nothing more than conglomerate chunks of cement plastered together in a military bunk-like fashion.

There were only a few vehicles on the road along with the bus. Compact cars blurred by, switching in and out of lanes, daring others to either yield or keep up. Spanish music and gangster rap booming from the speakers, tinted windows rolled halfway down, and smoke whispering out.

Sprawling convenience stores gave way to neglected

corner bodegas and liquor stores. Kids younger than Olive were lurking outside, desperate for some sort of action, anxiously staring down anything that crossed their vision. The old Omni Theater on the right was her cue to ring for her stop. The boarded-up windows hid the once overflowing talent that the historic theater hosted before she was born.

The sun was setting as Olive got off the bus. The humidity hit her like a brick wall. Olive clutched her bag tight to her side and kept her head down as she approached the Plaza Hotel. The sound of crunched broken glass synced up with her accelerating heartbeat. Random screams coming from inside the cracked walls of the hotel interrupted her interior dialogue.

The façade of the building looked more daunting to Olive than she last remembered. Graffiti was sprawled over every conceivable inch of the walls, giant bubbly nametags of people she never met nor wished to. Flashes of previous visits—weekends wasted on trying to do her homework amongst a room full of strange men, drug dealers, and a never-ending cloud of crack smoke—came rushing back to her as she climbed the steps to her mom's room.

The faded green carpet was still there. It resembled the

turf on the miniature golf course that she used to play on, years ago, with her mom. That was before the drugs took over. She had to step over empty boxes of discount wine and forty-ounce bottles of malt liquor just to get to the third floor. In front of her mother's room there was a man sitting on a lawn chair, reading a newspaper. He didn't pay Olive any attention until she reached for the doorknob. The gold numbers *312* in the middle of the door were rusty and dull.

"Hey little lady, where you think you going?"

"No, it's fine, I'm here to visit my mom."

The man stood up and faced Olive. She didn't know what to expect. His eyes looked unpredictable as they darted back and forth between her and the stairs she had just appeared from.

"What? You must be lost. Why don't you keep on moving along, there's nothing here for you."

"I'm looking for Grace, Grace Percival. She still lives here, right?"

The man dropped his paper and let out a loud sigh of annoyance. She didn't know if he was going to hit her or hug her. Neither option sounded comforting.

"Yeah, she's here." He stopped for a moment and gave

her the most menacing look he could conjure up. "Who are you?"

"I'm her daughter, Olive."

"Stay put," he said.

He banged on the numbers once before slivering inside. The door was cracked ajar long enough for an idle smoke ring to escape. Without warning the door swung open and the man from before appeared, arm in arm, with a scrawny middle-aged white man who eerily resembled Olive's History teacher.

"She owes me man, I want my money back!"

"This ain't Sears dude. What you think, she's got a money back guarantee or something?"

The man scurried off like a cockroach. He didn't want to be seen in this neighborhood during the day.

Grace slowly emerged from the dark room. Beady eyes, bruised arms, sweat dripping down her matted hair. She looked like a wounded animal. She let out a forced smile exposing the few teeth she had left, a combination of brown and yellow. Olive thought of bruised bananas and baked beans.

Grace nodded for her to enter the room. She remained at the edge of the doorway, her feet still on the beer-stained carpet in her room, not wanting to expose her fragile body to the humid air outside.

Before returning to his newspaper, the man approached Grace and spoke into her ear.

"Don't forget you got another client in an hour."

He gave Olive one more scan before closing the door behind her.

"Hey sweetie. How was the trip? You got all your stuff?"

Grace lit a cigarette on the wrong end.

"Watch it!"

"Calm down, it's only a smoke."

"Whatever. So, what's the deal, you have someone coming over soon or what?"

Grace scanned the room for the ashtray.

"Yeah, about that, do you mind maybe stepping out for a bit while mommy takes care of some business? You could go down the street and pick up some food."

Another night spent doing homework at the all-night White Castle. Probably less of a chance of catching something, Olive thought to herself as she brushed past the man guarding the door. He had already moved on to the Sports section as she reached the steps. He had no use for the local section, full of cryptic, unemotional crime reports. He was living it every day.

THAT MOMENT

That moment when I wake up in the morning and log into Facebook for the first time that day. Filled with childlike anticipation. But there are no new notifications. No friend requests, no messages, no invites, no likes, no comments; nothing. The lack of red at the top of the screen makes me feel isolated, alone. The blue bar is a reminder of how little I matter.

I log off, tell myself it's just Facebook, that it's no big deal, that it's virtual, that I should focus on tangible things in my real life, face-to-face relationships. I make a promise that I'll stay off for a week, nothing too drastic. I tried to deactivate my account before but there's a two-week period where you can reactivate. It was too enticing; I caved both times in less than 72 hours. On the fourth day I convince myself that I might be missing something important, some vital message that if unread for too long would be useless. The allure of the unknown reels me back in. When I log in, I try to guard my expectations, keep them realistic. I'll be fine with whatever notifications I get. I tell myself that it's about quality not quantity. As the screen loads, the excitement overcomes me once again.

Nothing but blue. I hit refresh every five seconds for the next minute but nothing changes. I feel empty inside, feel like when I was a child and I didn't get invited to a birthday party or a sleepover. It sounds trivial but it hurts, somewhere in the middle of my gut. Instead of remaining a victim, wallowing in my own sadness, I take a proactive approach. I begin by friend requesting anyone who has more than ten friends in common. Somehow that number seems acceptable. Then I go to my friends' pages, scroll through their timelines, and flip through their photos. I scour events, upcoming birthdays, anything I can think of. But nothing makes up for the lack of activity coming my way. I sit back and log off, realize that this whole thing, this whole exercise is fucked. I tell myself that it doesn't matter but it does. This is the same feeling, the closest metaphor that I can conjure up to describe my depression.

That moment when I log into Facebook and notice that a bunch of my friends are on as well and are available to chat. Amidst the clutter and activity of the first minute of being on, I don't start to chat. Instead I scroll around. I snoop around an ex's page or search for acquaintances from childhood. It's only after a few minutes of being on that I look back at the chat sidebar and all of them have signed off; at least the friends I consider my real friends, the ones I actually have a real life relationship with. It was almost instantaneous, this mass exodus of unavailable people all at the same time, all suddenly and mysteriously too busy to remain on chat. I rack my mind for possible reasons and excuses because I want to give them the benefit of the doubt, understanding that it's important not to make it all about me. But it's inevitable, this feeling that I caused this. The more I try to keep my mind off of it, the more it comes back to that sidebar on the bottom right, the lack of green dots next to my friends like a missile pointed directly at me.

One last experiment to confirm my suspicions. I log off, check my email, read some article to pass time. I log back in after a few minutes. Again, repeated the same as before. The chat goes back up to a few dozen and then within a minute it's down to single digits. It's official; this is all because of me. It has to be, right? The only thing worse than this, right here, right now, is when I start a conversation with one of my friends and he suddenly signs off, leaving my initial hello hanging in the chat box, empty, by itself. Now my mind is racing, it's in overdrive and there's nothing that's going to stop it. I'm on the wheel now, nothing more than a hamster in a cage. My mind is trying to analyze unseen things, picturing my friends at their computers, laughing at me. Feeling that social media is just some large plot to further ridicule those who are vulnerable and exacerbate the inevitable feelings of insecurity. This is the closest metaphor that I can conjure up to describe my anxiety and paranoia.

THE ARCHITECTURE OF AN EMPTY SKYLINE

The store was empty, except for a few older Hispanic men. They were huddled around the counter listening to the radio. When Wilson opened the door, the crowd didn't even turn to look at him. It was as if he were invisible. He liked this.

The aisles were crammed together, packed with out-of-date packages and cans that had a layer of dust on them. He grabbed a bag of pretzels and went to the back fridges. No overpriced foreign beers with fancy labels. Just obscure minority swill and crappy white trash beer. This was his type of place. Complete opposite of where Nancy used to take him. Coat and tie were always required and an American Express card was usually taken out. Now all he needed to get service were shoes and a shirt.

He grabbed three forties of Colt 45 and went to the front counter. A lone cockroach scrambled in front of his feet. Wilson was jealous of the critter's freedom. The two men on his side of the counter parted ways silently and let Wilson place his stuff in front of the cashier. The cashier looked at Wilson for a moment after looking down at the beer.

He smiled and mumbled to him, "Trying to have a good time?"

"Trying to forget about the bad times," he responded, and tossed the money towards the man.

The smile evaporated from the man's face as he handed Wilson the change.

The subway was empty. Instead of getting off at his usual stop, he continued to ride the train all the way down past the financial district. He couldn't quite face the scenes of his now former life. The brownstones with the yuppies quietly sitting down to relax for the evening. Happy families discussing the day's events with one another. It all seemed distant to him. His family, Nancy and their two kids, Skylar and Hope, were probably getting ready for bed. Nancy trying her best to groom them to be accustomed to nights without Daddy. The thought of reading them a bedtime story was too much for Wilson to deal with right now.

He wanted to be amongst the quietness of the skyscrapers. Since the divorce he had grown accustomed to the silence that now surrounded him. He got off at Wall Street and headed south. South Street was just a few blocks away, and by the time he got there, he had already finished a forty. As he walked towards the edge of the city, he began to feel overwhelmed by the greatness of the surrounding structures staring down at him from high above in the clear city night. He'd never been down here at this time of night. He was used to suits attached to their Blackberries, walking hurriedly in and out of buildings. Now it was just him and the gray structures. The few lit windows high above looked like eyes glaring down at him, teasing him with their ability to dominate the skyline.

The wind picked up considerably as he reached the water. The final forty was beginning to get warm by the time he opened it.

He moved towards the rubble of the World Trade Center.

He had been in bed with his secretary at the time. Nancy still had no idea as to what he had been doing. As much as he hated being a cliché, he couldn't resist the warm embrace of a younger woman's body. She had adored him. Maybe it was the money and power, the fact that he was her boss. He didn't care to know specifically.

By the time he had gotten home later that day, the news stations were all replaying live footage of the planes crashing into the towers. Nancy had been through enough just trying to get in touch with the kids and get them home from school. She'd probably fall apart if she knew of his indiscretions. He had used the devastation, the thousands of dead bodies, as an excuse to cover up his lies.

He was amazed at the enormity of the space. The sight frightened him, for he had never been so close to such a devastating scene. He could detect a faint trace of an odor. That could have been the gas and poison the news warned about. Whatever it was, Wilson coughed violently.

He looked up into the sky, trying to place the towers back into the clouds with his imagination. He stumbled on the sidewalk as he chased a handful of pills down with the last of the forty. He wondered if he was stepping over spots where people had landed after throwing themselves off the burning tower. He wished that the buildings were still there so that he could climb the steps and jump. That was the only way he could forgive himself for what had taken place, for the hole that he had created in his life and his heart.

A SIMPLE GESTURE

The plane's constant moans kept Francis and Anne awake for the entire trip. Francis wasn't going to sleep. He had paperwork to look through, documents to sign. Anne had a miniature-sized cocktail and began flipping through glossy, trashy celebrity magazines. It was her one guilty pleasure. She felt safe up here, off of the ground. Safe enough in her anonymity amongst fellow travelers, faceless people she'd likely never see again, to blatantly indulge in her mindless hobby.

Every few pages she'd glance over at Francis. She was amazed at him. Everything about him, his posture, his ability to remain still for hour after hour, doing nothing after he put away the papers except stare out the window into the dark, endless night, amazed his wife. Anne herself was visibly giddy with excitement for their arrival and the beginning of their vacation. She was also jealous, but in a good way. She longed for his patience and his certainty that what he was doing was right in moments such as this. Anne wanted that and more from Francis. At the start of their relationship she'd gone out with him just to feel his energy vibrating off of him. She wanted to catch some of it, to somehow bottle it up and better herself, awaken herself because of it. Over the years, through everything, that energy hadn't ceased. Instead, it had grown stronger, and Anne loved her husband for that above all else.

Of course it wasn't a vacation to Francis. Sure, he could enjoy parts of the summer that lay before him. Moments of isolated solitude with just him and his wife, enjoying a quiet breakfast in the city or a postcard view of the countryside on a weekend trip, but those would be few and far between. His silence, although fooling his wife into a speechless admiration of him, was more of a muzzled energy that he turned inward, analyzing everything that he had to do once he touched down.

This trip wasn't a job to Francis; it was more, much more. It was a chance to reshape the economic and environmental future of his ancestral homeland. Up until now, Francis had gone about his career with the acquisition of wealth serving as his guiding light. That certainty was his solace. The unceasing quality and value of money stabilized Francis in times of personal upheaval. Through hair lost, waistline expansion, even the death of loved ones, Francis could always rely on his never-ending quest to try and obtain more money. This goal was, at first, an attempt at the American dream, to provide his family with more comfort than he'd had growing up. It somehow morphed over the years. It was now a part of his personality; it was what made him feel whole, what got him out of bed in the morning. To resist this urge, to accept this job *pro bono* and take on all of the expenses of the summer as an out-of-pocket loss (which he could well afford), was a defining moment in Francis' life. He'd found a new mission thirty thousand feet above sea level, over the dark, cold waters of the Atlantic.

The only time Francis' posture changed was towards the end of the flight. Just before the pilot came on and announced to prepare for landing, Anne noticed Francis' eyes flutter at the sight out the window. It was early morning and the air outside the window had gone from a dark, uninviting blue that looked like a day-old bruise after a fistfight to a light hue of powder blue, sprinkled with rays of warm orange coming from the few slits in the large, fluffy clouds from which light could escape.

Anne leaned in to try and share in the vision. She could still remember the first time she saw the west coast of Ireland. Its rolling green hills resembled a vast, never-ending quilt with its patchwork of different versions of green. She never knew one color could have so many variations. That was before they were married. No kids, fewer responsibilities.

Now, with more than a dozen trips behind her, she took in the color and the quilt came to mind, but the land, the vision, had more to offer her now. That quilt, once just a beautiful view, now had a story behind it. She'd heard parts of the story on her trips, around the fireplace at the pubs late at night in between songs or back at the cousin's country farmhouse around dinner. She'd felt the knee-high walls separating Francis' family's farm from their neighbors. The cold, jagged rocks were stacked haphazardly. She once asked why there were no large farms like back home. Francis looked at his feet. She detected a pinch of shame in his eyes.

"Because that's all the Queen allowed them to have."

Only in the early morning fog of one too many Guinnesses did he open up a bit more. Stories told of shared pasts, a common struggle. Anne didn't share; she had no tales to tell. She listened, devoured it all. Each and every story. The famine. The wars and revolutions. The imprisonments. The struggle to somehow legitimize an entire people through government policies. The religious clashes. The anger now turned to guilt and shame. The repression of their native tongue in their own schools. The drunken revisionist debates over which leader to follow— Collins or de Valera. There was no wrong answer; there were only deeply personal allegiances. That much Anne was sure of.

As they approached the coast, she gently rubbed up against Francis, resting at the base of his neck, just under the beginning of his stubble. She caught a glimpse of the coastline. That was enough for now. She had the entire summer. She focused on Francis. He hadn't blinked since land came into view. At that moment, as her husband leaned his head up against the small glass window, faintly touching it with two of his fingers as he tried desperately to reach out and touch the beauty below, Anne knew that he was full. Full of joy, full of gratitude, full, for the first time in his adult life, just full of life.

Before they touched down, making the journey complete and tangible, Anne's appreciation of her husband's contentment instantly vanished and was replaced by a deep, sharp feeling of guilt and loneliness. Maybe it was the other couples surrounding them, sharing in the excitement of anticipation, almost bursting at the thought of opening the door and setting foot on Irish soil, or maybe it was the barely audible conversations: the mutual appreciation of the moment shared. Anne sat in silence. The seatbelt felt tight, constricting, locking her into place like the obedient partner she was. As Francis remained unmoved, his entire attention devoted to the bleak early morning view of the airport tarmac, Anne wanted to scream. Scream out to him, to remind him that she was there. That it was okay, somehow necessary, to communicate his feelings with her and make sure she was enjoying herself.

This wasn't her trip; nothing about this summer was hers. She realized the childishness of her emotions, which nonetheless were real and growing by the moment. His demeanor reeked of a lack of fulfillment, making it difficult to penetrate. He'd built a wall around himself and she couldn't intrude. In times like these Francis reminded Anne of her father. His silence, especially in his later years, paralyzed the entire household, holding her mother hostage. She wasn't going to let that happen to her. The plane finally stopped rolling, idling in place at the desired gate. Anne sat back and tried to let her feelings pass. This was important to her husband so, in turn, it was important to her. It should be that way; it had to be that way. Made things easier.

As much as she wanted to take in the moment, own it somehow like Francis, something wasn't right. She knew what the summer held for her. Lone trips to used bookstores, museums, and historical sites. One ticket for plays, tables for one at small, family-owned side street cafés. Before leaving she had known that this was a business trip for Francis, but something about it finally clicked in at that moment. The loneliness that she was feeling was understandable. Anne took comfort in the rationality of her feeling, her ability to work through it by herself.

The next three months would be the crowning of a life's worth of being a plus one. Anne's value was tied to the men in her life. Handed from her father on her wedding day to Francis. The old man silently nodding in the groom's direction, signifying the unspoken transfer of modern-day patriarchal ownership. She'd play the dutiful, happy wife. For his sake. His needs were paramount. Always had been. Anne recognized the imbalance in their marriage, but this wasn't the place to bring forth her argument for change.

She grabbed her bag from the overhead storage compartment and prepared to leave the plane. Francis grabbed her bag in one swift motion. No smile, no sincere declaration of manners, just a simple act. Anne soaked in the moment, trying to hold onto it, somehow freeze it, hoping that it would be enough to last until his next gesture.

ACKNOWLEDGMENTS

The following stories, in different and earlier forms, have previously appeared in the following publications:

"Superhero" — *Bartleby Snopes*

"Accidental Memories" — *WordPlaySound*

"One Hit Wonder" — *TwentySomething Press*

"A Promise Is Nothing More than a Future Regret"
— *FRXTL*

I'd like to thank my publisher and editor, Greg Pece, for his tireless work. His revisions, suggestions, and thoughtful insights turned the manuscript into a book. I couldn't have done it without his watchful eye and careful guidance.

ABOUT THE AUTHOR

PATRICK TROTTI is the author of a novella, *The Day The Cloud Stood Still* (Ever Books/Pteron Press), and a mixed-genre chapbook, *Fracture(d)* (Bottlecap Press). His short fiction and poetry have appeared in dozens of literary magazines and journals, both in print and online. He lives in Tarrytown, New York, where he is a freelance writer, editor, and avid baseball fan.